THE AFFAIR

N. A. COOPER

BLOODHOUND
— BOOKS —

First published in 2023 by Bloodhound Books.

www.bloodhoundbooks.com

Print ISBN: 978-1-5040-8625-7

For my sisters.
My best friends.

CHAPTER ONE

AFTER

The early morning sun settled on the loch, the uncertain skies of dawn reflecting in its inky surface. Alex's skin tingled as the water held her, her legs kicking out at the things she could not see. The sound of the gentle lapping of the current filled her ears; she kicked harder, keeping her head above the surface. A couple of wading birds dipped in and out nearby, their calls echoing off the mountains.

It was a cool morning, the low sun bright but deceptive – an illusion, Alex thought, there to light up the land and nothing more. She could hear the Highland breeze whispering among the harsh landscape, disturbing the undergrowth and racing through the trees. The icy water continued to bite at her skin; it never warmed here regardless of the heat from the sun – the loch was too big and it held too much – but it never iced over either; it was simply always cold. Alex liked the consistency of it. The predictability. It felt stable in a way that nothing else did, unaffected by the things which come and go.

Alex's chest stung but she stayed focused, the water lapping gently around her neck and her eyes set on the cabin in front of her. It stood just beyond the shoreline, slightly elevated in the shadows cast by the ash trees which flanked it, their spindly limbs reaching out towards each other. The calls of the birds accompanied her as they always did, their songs washing over her like the water. Her legs continued to kick out beneath her, keeping her afloat, but her eyes never left the cabin.

The surface of the loch was visible in her line of sight, stretching out like oil before her. Patches of reed cast shadows beneath, darkness lurking among the beauty. She took a deep breath, the cool air catching in her throat, her chest expanding. She held it there for a moment then exhaled slowly, watching as it caused ripples on the water in front of her. This was *her* time – a moment she'd become accustomed to before he woke. The routine anchored her in a way she needed and it became as vital to her as the oxygen she breathed.

Her watch beeped – the ten minutes were over. She swam back to the pebbly shore, her feet finding the bed of the loch and the stones which protruded awkwardly from it. She walked to the cabin and climbed the set of steps to the wooden decking, damp tracks marking her path to the plastic table and chairs at the far end. She grabbed the towel she'd left there and wrapped it around her shoulders before sitting.

Her feet were numb; she clenched and unclenched her toes, trying to regain feeling. Her eyes swept the loch, left to right, but she saw only what it was willing to show her. The sun was rising in no particular hurry, the silhouette of the mountains reflecting in the mirror-like surface of Ness. She felt her heart rate returning to normal, her chest loosening. Her skin still prickled, the usual paleness tinged with red. She tied the towel around her waist and wrung out her hair, then she padded barefoot into the cabin to make herself a drink.

The bedroom door was open a fraction – just enough that she could see through it. She moved towards it, the palm of her hand holding the wall and her nose almost touching the door. He was still asleep, his hair almost black against the white sheets, his arm resting above his head and his chest rising and falling in rhythm.

She turned quietly, careful not to wake him, and dropped the damp towel onto one of the chairs. She made herself a coffee and slipped into her robe before tiptoeing back outside onto the decking. She would watch the sun rise over the loch; she liked watching the way it crept above the mountains and lit a narrow path of orange across its surface. Soon, that narrow strip would turn into a blazing fire of red and gold. She sat down and propped her feet up on the chair opposite, taking in the view. It never failed to consume her – the raw untamed beauty of it.

She'd always been an early riser. Her favourite time of day was dawn, when the sky echoed her own uncertainty. It was neither night nor day, light nor dark; the grey space between the two provided her with a simple comfort she couldn't explain. The world woke slowly, the birds loud but the people quiet, the gentle rhythm of the water soothing her mind and helping to wash away the nightmares that always lingered long after dark. But no matter how long she sat there or how mesmerised she became by the sound of it, a trace of the torment would always remain, an echo of something she tried to forget but knew she never would.

Her eyes glanced back towards the door where inside he slept – a night owl rather than an early riser like her. She cradled the mug in her hands and held it close to her chest, the steam rising and warming her cheeks. Her toes were still numb and her hair tangled and damp, occasional droplets of water tracing the length of her spine.

It was going to be a nice day, she could tell by the sky already clearing – the sun would warm up and the clouds would disappear. It was as if the water knew too; it seemed to shimmer and glisten in anticipation. She breathed in the earthy smells of the forest and watched as a red squirrel appeared from a thicket of trees. It froze, staring at Alex, then a moment later two babies appeared; it picked one up in its mouth and led the other back into the treeline.

Alex sipped her coffee and watched as the wildlife awakened. Further down the shoreline a heron stood tall and graceful among the undergrowth, its sleekness at odds with its rugged surroundings. Alex liked spotting them, their statuesque patience as they waited for their breakfast to arrive at their feet. In the evenings, she would look out at the loch in the fading light and wonder what lurked beneath its surface. What secrets did Ness have? Was there a monster in there somewhere?

She heard a rustle from the trees beside her, a crunching of the leaves. Her head was turned before she'd even realised which direction it had come from. She saw the branches of an ash tree swaying, the leaves vibrating from the sudden unseen force. She stood, the chair scraping against the decking and her hands grasping the wooden railing. Was there something there? Or someone?

Her eyes narrowed as she tried to make out any movement, but there was nothing. It was just her imagination, ignited by the things that would forever haunt her. It was draining, always expecting something to go wrong. It exhausted her mind and then her body. The cold water therapy helped but it couldn't cure the ingrained sense of panic she'd grown accustomed to feeling, the adrenaline that coursed through her veins at the slightest hint of something amiss. She found a certain degree of solace in acknowledging that, on some level, her body was prepared. She finished her coffee and went inside.

The room was one open-plan space, the kitchen diner meeting with the lounge. The only thing that distinguished between the two was the change in flooring, cheap linoleum meeting a threadbare beige carpet. The place was furnished when she'd arrived; it wasn't to her taste, but it was home. The walls were wood panelled with large paintings hung at odd intervals; some depicting the loch, others focused on the wildlife. She'd intended to take the paintings down when she first arrived; she could recall squinting at them through blurry eyes, hating them for portraying the world in all its beauty.

She'd forgotten at first, bogged down by the more pressing issues of relocating over four hundred miles with little planning, but as the weeks passed by she found that they'd grown on her. She turned on the kitchen light and, as she did, the glow illuminated something out on the decking, something that wasn't there before. The silhouette of someone lurking, moving slowly towards the door. Alex froze, the panic paralysing her for a moment too long.

She'd left the door unlocked.

She ran. Ran across the room towards the door, bumping into a chair and tripping on her bag, her arms outstretched. She cleared the space as quick as she could, but the panic had cost her valuable seconds. The door handle moved and, without seeing who it was, she knew.

She knew who had come for her.

For *them.*

CHAPTER TWO

BEFORE

Alex sat at the bar cradling a cold bottle of beer in her hands. David had left almost an hour earlier but she'd decided to stay for another drink by herself; she didn't have anywhere else to go on a Saturday night and the alcohol was helping her to forget the awful date she'd just endured.

On paper, David was a perfect match for her. He'd been single for over a year; he had his own place; he enjoyed keeping fit and spending time outdoors; he wanted to travel, and was looking for someone to join him. They'd been matched on a dating website and had spent three weeks exchanging messages before he'd asked her out. He'd been easy to talk to over WhatsApp – interesting and intelligent and all of the other traits she was looking for in a man. And on top of all that, he'd seemed genuinely interested in her.

In reality, David was dull, and what he lacked in personality he made up for in arrogance. She knew within the first five minutes that it wasn't going to work out, but her ingrained need to be polite had forced her to sit and ride out the two hours of awkward silences and boring conversation that followed. She couldn't work out how she'd managed to read him so wrong.

When David suggested going back to his place, she'd pretended to stifle a yawn and said she couldn't, that she was exhausted and had to be up early the next day. She didn't say why, and he didn't ask. She was mortified: he hadn't even *tried* to hide his intentions. They split the bill and David got his phone out, making alternative plans she had no interest in.

'Another?' asked the barman. She'd drained the last of her beer without noticing and sat idly skimming the top of the bottle with her forefinger. She checked the time – just after ten. The bar was getting busier, the Saturday night crowds masking the music.

'Please.' She would have one more then call for a taxi. Maybe she'd order takeout on the way home, enough so she could save some for breakfast the next day. She had a feeling she was going to wake up with a sore head and a desire for something greasy.

The barman took the empty bottle away and replaced it with a fresh one, a slice of lime sticking out of the top. She pushed it in with her finger and watched the lime fizz as it dropped, her eyes focusing on the bubbles until her vision began to blur.

'Hello.' A voice to her right made her jump; she turned to find a man leaning on the bar next to her – she recognised him but couldn't recall his name. Something Blake. His daughter was in her class – Mia Blake. She swallowed hard and tried to regain herself, to shake the fog from her mind 'Miss Vaughn,' he said, smiling.

'Mr Blake, hi! Sorry, I was miles away.'

'Ryan,' he said, holding out his hand. 'I don't think we've ever officially been introduced.' Alex shook his hand; it seemed oddly formal. They'd met several times at school – Ryan dropped Mia off on Mondays and Fridays and occasionally picked her up in the week, but they'd never had much reason to exchange anything other than pleasantries before. 'Mia loves you!'

Alex tried to force her mind to formulate something to say; she was acutely aware that she'd drunk too much and was desperately trying not to let it show. She wasn't used to seeing parents in this situation. Usually, she was stood at the gate welcoming the children into school, answering a stream of questions or passing information over to mums and dads at the end of the day. She prided herself on always being professional. She'd seen parents outside of school before but never while intoxicated. She wasn't sure what she should do or how she should act. Should she leave? She didn't want to seem rude. She looked after this man's daughter all day, the least she could do was be polite.

'She's a joy to have in the class, you must be very proud.'

'Thank you, I am. Can I get you a drink?'

'I'm fine, thank you. I'm just finishing this one then I'm going to get a taxi home.'

The barman appeared and Ryan turned to him. 'Just a Coke please, mate. Are you waiting for someone?' he asked Alex, gesturing to the empty stool beside her.

'No.' Alex felt her cheeks flush. She felt as though she'd been caught doing something shameful, the empty space beside her accounting for a gaping hole in her life she couldn't seem to fill.

'Mind if I sit and keep you company?' Alex didn't know what to say, her mouth opened but no words came out. 'Sorry, am I intruding?'

'Oh no, it's not that... I'm just not sure how it would look should anyone see us.'

He looked around, grinning. 'I don't think the parents at school are the type to be on a night out in the city.'

'No, you're probably right.'

Ryan sat down as the barman placed his drink in front of him; he paid then turned back to Alex. 'So how did you end up working in Elwood?'

'I grew up there.'

'Really?' Ryan smiled as though amused by this.

'Yeah, I went to that school as a child.'

'I didn't have you down as a country girl.'

Alex couldn't help but laugh. 'At heart, I am. I grew up near the woods. My parents still live there, actually.' She took a sip of her beer.

'So why did you move?'

'University mainly, but I couldn't move back to my parents after the freedom of the city. Have you any idea how nice it is to be able to go out past eight at night and find things are still open?'

'I did it the opposite way to you. I grew up in Sheffield, right on the edge of the city. I couldn't wait to get away from it all.'

'Really, why?'

'I hated the constant noise and the chaos. Everywhere was always busy. In Elwood, you can walk for hours without seeing a single person.'

'That's true. I once got lost in those woods.'

'You did?' Ryan grinned, clearly wanting to know more.

'Yep. Most terrifying few hours of my life. It was the first time I was allowed out on my own, I must have been around nine or ten. I packed some snacks and a drink into my little backpack and went off on an adventure.'

'Oh dear.'

'I quickly realised I didn't know those woods as well as I'd thought I did. Worst thing was, no one even realised I was missing. *Three* hours I was gone. When I turned up at home my mum wondered why I was all puffy eyed. When I told her she just laughed.' Alex shrugged. 'Village people,' she said, rolling her eyes.

'Yeah, they're a different breed, that's for sure.'

'And everyone knows everyone's business in Elwood. You can't have secrets.' She took another drink and felt it clouding her mind. She pushed the bottle away from her.

'Ah, so you moved to the city to keep your skeletons in their closet?'

'Something like that. For privacy, I guess. And for the late-night takeout.'

Ryan laughed. 'So, what are you doing out on your own on a Saturday night?'

'What are *you* doing out on your own on a Saturday night?'

'Touché!' He took a drink and thought about it for a moment. 'I needed some space. Decided to have a drive out.'

'Ah.' She didn't want to pry but she had to admit she was curious. Space from who? His wife? 'I had a date that ended about an hour ago.'

'Didn't go too well then?'

Alex shook her head. 'Do they ever?'

'I've had my fair share of bad dates. What happened?'

'Oh nothing, but that's the problem. It was just...' Alex thought for a moment, trying to find the right word. 'Unexceptional.'

'Unexceptional?'

'Yeah, you know... ordinary. Plain. Average.'

'But who wants average, huh?'

'Exactly. I want... *sparks.* Oh God, I sound like a hopeless romantic, don't I?'

'What's wrong with that?'

Alex sighed. 'I'm starting to think...' She trailed off, beginning to question whether she was divulging too much.

'What?'

'I'm starting to think I'll never meet anyone. I'll be one of those old spinster women with loads of cats. And I hate cats.'

Ryan laughed. 'You just have to find the right person.'

'That's what everyone says. But what if...' she stopped herself, some sober remnant of her mind reminding her not to say the things she would admonish herself for the next day, when a clear mind and a crippled conscience would make her feel worse than the hangover.

'What if the right person doesn't exist?' Ryan finished her sentence for her, looking at her with narrowing eyes, as though he was trying to see the things she wanted to hide.

Alex shrugged. 'Maybe.' At the back of her mind, blurry and muffled, her sober self was screaming at her to stop talking, to remain professional and leave. She knew she shouldn't be discussing her personal life with the parent of one of her students, and yet at the same time, the intoxicated part of herself was wanting to open up to this man, to tell him her deepest fears and hope that he would be able to alleviate them. 'That's what it feels like sometimes, anyway.'

'That's what everyone thinks, until they don't anymore. The right person could be just around the corner or they could be some distance away, but they're there.'

'What makes you so sure?'

He turned away for a moment and looked into his drink as though it could provide him with answers. Alex watched him, his long eyelashes and his bright blue eyes; the way his cheeks dimpled when he smiled; the gold band on his left hand.

'Just a feeling,' he said. 'You're a good catch, and Mia is a good judge of character.'

Alex pulled her beer back towards her, taking one last drink; she had to leave, the mention of Mia had brought her back to reality. This was her student's *father*. The repercussions of embarrassing herself in front of Ryan were suddenly laid out for her in her mind. 'I'd better be going.'

She lowered herself off of the stool and grabbed her bag from the bar. As she turned she felt a wave of dizziness that caused her to wobble, the world suddenly unstable. Her hands grasped for something solid and found Ryan's arm. He stood beside her and placed a hand on the small of her back, steadying her.

'Hey, you okay?'

'I'm so sorry, this is really unprofessional of me. I haven't had that much to drink but I'm not used to it and I haven't eaten...' The excuses came flowing out of her, trying to mask her embarrassment.

'Don't be so hard on yourself, it's the weekend.'

'I should go.'

'Don't be silly, let me drive you home.'

'Oh no, I couldn't...'

'I'm not putting you in a taxi on your own, so you either let me drive you home or I'll have to take a taxi with you to yours and then back again, which seems daft.'

Alex tried to gather herself, to weigh up the pros and cons and determine what she should do, but despite her best efforts she couldn't seem to make a decision. As though answering her uncertainty, Ryan placed his hand on her arm and guided her out of the bar. She let him, feeling his hand move from her arm to her back; the weight of it strong yet gentle, a man leading her in a way she hadn't experienced in a long time.

A cool wind greeted them outside. Alex crossed her arms over her chest and held herself close, Ryan's hand still hovering at her back as they walked.

'I'm parked around the corner.' He gestured up ahead to Williamson Street where a little car park sat behind a shop. 'Fresh air helping?'

She took a deep breath as though checking. 'Yes, I think so. I'm sorry about this, I'm so embarrassed.'

'Don't be. You're not on duty all the time, at the weekends you have to switch off Miss Vaughn and let... actually, I don't know your name?'

'Alex.'

'Alex,' he echoed, as though trying it out. He looked at her, the street lights reflecting in his bright blue eyes. 'At the weekends, you have to let Alex out.'

'Maybe so, but I'd really appreciate your discretion. I don't relish the thought of being talked about on the playground.'

'This might surprise you, Alex, but I don't spend my free time gossiping with other mums and dads...'

'Oh you don't? I'm shocked!' She grinned at him as they walked side by side, turning into the car park on the right-hand side of the street. It was poorly lit and the darkness seemed to welcome them, masking things which they both knew mattered. 'What about Hannah?'

'What about her?'

'I can't ask you not to tell her but...' she trailed off, hoping he would pick up her meaning. She didn't want him to tell his wife he'd bumped into their five-year-old daughter's teacher on a night out, drinking alone after a failed date, but if he had to, she would prefer Hannah kept it to herself.

'Don't worry, we're not exactly on good terms at the moment, the last thing I want to do is make things worse by telling her I took an attractive and *slightly* inebriated woman home. Even if she is our child's teacher.'

Alex felt her heart flutter at his words and, just like that, she was thirteen again, at the school disco when Jay Weaver had asked her to dance and said that he liked her dress.

Ryan took out his keys and pointed them towards a car parked over in the corner. The indicators flashed as it unlocked. 'Sorry,' he said, his forehead creasing. 'I shouldn't have said that, it's just... things aren't great at home.' He stopped walking and turned to face her.

'I'm sorry to hear that.'

'Would it be wildly inappropriate to tell you I had a good time tonight?'

Alex opened her mouth but the words wouldn't come. Her heart was telling her to respond one way while her head was telling her to say something else entirely. She was conflicted, suspended in a moment of confusion she couldn't seem to break free from. Ryan took a step towards her and brushed a strand of hair away from her face.

'We can't... we shouldn't...' she stuttered. She felt so small next to him, his frame eclipsing her, making her feel simultaneously safe and on edge. Her eyes flittered around the car park – they were alone, but exposed. She could hear the hustle and bustle of the Saturday night crowds passing on the high street less than two hundred metres away. There were so many conflicting emotions searing through her body; she didn't know which to listen to and which to ignore. It was wrong and unprofessional, yet exciting and spontaneous.

Ryan bent down towards her, his eyes holding hers, his fingertips grazing her arms. 'I know, I know,' he whispered.

Before Alex knew what was happening they were kissing, his mouth warm on hers and his fingers entangled in her hair, pulling her into him. He smelled good. He *felt* good. She kept telling herself to stop but her body wasn't listening. She wanted him, and she felt powerless.

CHAPTER THREE

Alex stepped back, creating space between them that should never have been closed in the first place. 'That shouldn't have happened.'

'Shit. I'm sorry. That was my fault.' Ryan ran his fingers through his hair and then along his jawline, his eyes full of regret. He turned away from her and looked towards his car; Alex wondered whether he was thinking about leaving her like this, running away from his mistake. It made her feel dirty, the fact that she had allowed herself to become someone's transgression.

'I should go,' she said.

'No, please, don't do that. I feel terrible enough already. Let me drive you home then we can forget all about this, okay?'

Alex looked over her shoulder towards the high street. She could walk back there, call a cab and pretend none of this happened, but she knew that leaving it like this would send questions spinning through her mind for a long time to come. She wouldn't tell anyone, she knew that, but she wanted to be certain that he wouldn't either.

'Okay. I live in New Brook; do you know it?'

Ryan nodded. They walked towards his car in silence and

Alex got into the passenger side. In the back, she could see Mia's car seat and a doll sat inside it. On the seat next to it was a pink backpack and a colouring book. Sweet little Mia – how could Alex have done this?

Ryan started the engine and reversed out of the parking bay. The headlights scanned the car park and Alex was relieved to see there was no one around. She lowered herself in the seat as they passed through the high street, making herself as small as possible, hiding the best she could. She felt Ryan glance at her and increase his speed until they were away from the crowds.

Alex sat back up. 'We can't tell anyone what happened.'

'Yeah, we're on the same page about that.'

'Good.'

'I'm sorry, I don't know what I was thinking. I'm a married man, I've never done anything like that before.'

Alex wasn't sure whether it was intentional but his words made her feel even worse; as if she needed a reminder that he was married. 'So we just pretend this never happened, okay?'

'Okay. But for what it's worth, I meant what I said earlier. You're a good catch. You'll find someone.'

Alex laughed but it was empty and hollow.

'What's so funny?' he asked.

'It's just one of those things people like you say to people like me.'

Alex felt Ryan looking at her, his eyes flitting back and forth between her and the road. She turned to see him frowning, the intermittent glow of the street lamps casting their light into the car. 'People like me?'

'People who are married. People who haven't had to join dating websites. I mean, have you ever had to endure speed dating? Or a blind date?' Alex regretted what she was saying before she'd finished. It made her sound bitter – a woman scorned – and that wasn't who she was. At least she didn't think so.

'I met Hannah when I was sixteen. I was at a friend's party celebrating the end of school when she turned up. We were together for eleven years before we separated. She wanted to get married and have kids and I... well, I felt like I'd been missing out. A couple of years later we bumped into each other at a mutual friend's wedding. One thing led to another and she ended up pregnant.'

'Oh...'

'Yes. Oh. I don't ever regret what happened, because without that night I wouldn't have Mia. But sometimes it's easy to forget that people *like me* haven't always got the fairy tale you might think.'

Alex didn't respond. She couldn't find the words. Ryan eased out across a roundabout and Alex saw the turn off to her road looming up ahead.

'I'm just up here.' Alex pointed to the left, a new-build estate just outside of Nottingham. Ryan indicated and turned in. 'Right at the end.'

'How long have you lived here?'

'A couple of years.'

He reached the end of the road and came to a stop in front of her building, where eight apartments branched off of a central hallway over two storeys.

'Which one's yours?' he asked.

She pointed through the window to the top left, where a little table and two chairs sat on the balcony, dragonfly shaped solar lights adorning the top of the railings.

'Nice place.'

'Yeah, small but plenty of room for me.'

He switched the engine off and turned in his seat to face her. 'I'm really sorry about tonight. I hope you won't hold it against me.'

'Of course not.'

'It's just… well, I felt something between us and I got carried away. I shouldn't have.'

At a loss for words, Alex simply nodded. She wasn't sure whether she was agreeing or just accepting this was how he felt, but she knew that if she sat in the car with him for much longer her resolve would weaken. She'd felt something between them too, something she hadn't felt in a long time.

'Thank you for the lift.' Alex opened the door and stepped out into the cool night air, the security light turning on as she moved closer to the front door. She took her keys out of her bag and turned to look at Ryan. He hadn't started the engine yet, he just sat watching her, a sad smile on his face. She couldn't work out whether it was regret or pity – or maybe a mixture of both. Did he feel sorry for her, going home to an empty house?

She stepped inside and shook her head, trying to dislodge the thought. He would drive home to his family, to his little girl tucked up in bed and his wife who he had just betrayed. Would he check in on Mia? Would Hannah wake as he crawled into bed?

Once Alex was inside her apartment, she went over to the French doors which overlooked the front of the block. She separated the blinds slightly so as not to be seen and peered out onto the road. She could see Ryan's car driving away, approaching the junction. He indicated right, pulling straight out onto the main road. She was about to step away when she noticed another vehicle – it approached slowly from the side of the building where Alex parked her car, then sped up the road towards the junction. She watched the dark hatchback indicated right and joined the main road, driving off in the same direction as Ryan and disappearing from view.

CHAPTER FOUR

A lex stood in the classroom trying to drain her mug of coffee before the children arrived, swiftly followed by the inevitable chaos of the morning routine. The weekend had taken its toll on her and when her alarm had gone off at six that morning she could barely open her eyes. It wasn't like her. She'd cut her usual run short by a couple of kilometres and instead spent the extra ten minutes in the shower.

Despite spending most of Sunday on the sofa watching TV, she still felt hungover. Her head was filled with a cloud she chose to attribute to the alcohol rather than her indiscretions – it was easier that way, blaming something other than herself. She hadn't been able to sleep properly since Saturday and her head was heavy with fatigue.

Parents were beginning to arrive. Alex stood watching them from the classroom window, the blinds still closed, a tiny slither of the playground outside visible at the edge. She took a last sip of her coffee, placed the mug on her desk and quickly checked her reflection in the little compact mirror she kept in her drawer. She knew Ryan would be dropping Mia off and she'd lost a bit of respect for herself for applying more make-up than usual because of it.

'I'm here, I'm here, sorry I'm late!' Alex's colleague Chloe came rushing through the internal door looking harassed, her breathing laboured. 'Had to drop Nora off at my mum's, she's been throwing up all night.'

Great, thought Alex. The last thing she needed was a sickness bug making its way around the classroom.

'Oh dear, poor Nora. And poor *you*, you must be shattered.'

Chloe stifled a yawn, nodding. 'You look nice this morning.'

Alex had chosen a navy-blue wrap dress from her wardrobe that morning which she wouldn't usually wear for work; it skimmed her curves and fitted in all the right places. 'Thank you. Come on, we'd better open up.'

Alex opened the front door and together they made their way down the ramp and through the play area sectioned off from the rest of the schoolyard by a little gate.

'Morning, everyone!' Alex called out, opening the gate and standing back to let the children in.

'I drew a picture for you, Miss Vaughn.' Logan handed her a drawing of something she couldn't quite make out, his name written at the bottom in bright red ink. He had a big smile on his face as she examined it, eagerly awaiting her response.

'This is wonderful, Logan. I'll put this up behind my desk! Off you go, follow Mrs Kensington.'

Chloe greeted the children and walked with them up the ramp and into the classroom while Alex held back, waiting for the inevitable barrage of questions and comments from the parents before they left.

'Miss Vaughn, Isla's complaining of a tummy ache, could you keep an eye on her?'

'Of course!' Alex smiled, tilting her head to one side as Isla passed, her long blonde hair in plaits and a frown on her face.

'Feeling a little under the weather? Just come and tell me if it gets any worse, okay?'

Before she'd finished talking Alex could hear a woman speaking over her, trying to get her attention. Alex turned to a woman on her left with a baby strapped to her chest in a sling. She looked like she hadn't brushed her hair and there was a stain on her shoulder which Alex suspected was sick. 'Finley's got an appointment on Friday so he won't be in school.' She turned to walk away but Alex shouted her back.

'Mrs Daniels, could you let the office know, please?'

She sighed. 'Will do.'

'Morning!' Alex's heart sank. Ryan was walking towards her holding Mia's hand – she looked upset, a stuffed rabbit clutched to her chest. Ryan's bright blue eyes fixed on Alex. 'You okay?' he asked.

The rest of the parents had begun to disperse, just a few stragglers chatting as they walked towards the school gates, occasionally looking back to wave to their children. Alex suddenly caught herself, regaining her composure and forcing a smile back onto her face.

'Yes. Yes I'm okay, thank you. Good morning, Mia, are you coming in to join the class?'

'She's feeling a little tearful, aren't you, Mia?' Ryan knelt down beside her and tucked her hair behind her ear. 'Miss Vaughn is going to look after you today, and Daddy will see you after school, okay?'

Fresh tears began to fall and Mia's lip trembled.

'Come on, Mia, you can help me do the register if you like? I can find you one of those sparkly stickers you love.'

'How does that sound?' Ryan's smile never left his face. No matter how terrible he was feeling about his little girl being upset, or how awkward he felt at seeing Alex, he never showed it. Mia nodded and he kissed her on the tip of her nose. It made Alex's heart melt. 'That's my girl!'

'Come on, Mia, let's get your bag hung up inside, shall we?' Alex reached out her hand but Mia hesitated before taking it.

'Actually, can I have a quick word?' Ryan stood with his hands in his pockets, a pale grey shirt tucked into a pair of black trousers. He was clean-shaven with his dark hair brushed back off his face and a lanyard hanging loosely around his neck. Alex tried not to look at the way his shirt pulled taut over his muscles; she tried not to remember the way it felt to be held in those arms or the way his mouth felt on hers.

'Of course.' She turned towards the classroom and saw that Chloe had reappeared in the doorway. 'Mrs Kensington, could you help Mia hang her bag up, please?'

'Absolutely! Come on, Mia, your rabbit can sit at the front today.'

Alex turned back to Ryan, her heart drumming and her palms sweating. She hated the effect he had on her; it made her feel completely out of control – a feeling that would no doubt be exciting and exhilarating given different circumstances. She tried her best to appear confident and professional. She'd spent the previous day considering how to handle things with Ryan and she'd decided she'd pretend as though nothing had happened; she needed to reassert her professional boundaries and keep the conversation strictly on Mia. But stood in front of him and weakening under his gaze, she suddenly seemed to forget everything.

'I wanted to apologise again for what happened the other night.' He kept his voice low and his expression serious, but there was something in his eyes, a playfulness that Alex tried to ignore.

'Not necessary. All forgotten, remember?' She kept her tone clipped and devoid of emotion.

Ryan nodded sheepishly. 'It's just… I haven't been able to stop thinking about you.'

A child came running across the playground towards them,

his mum pushing a pram in his wake, trying to catch up. 'I'm sorry we're late! The baby needed changing as we were leaving.'

'No problem at all. Good morning, Freddie.' She turned back to face Ryan. 'I'll keep an eye on Mia today, Mr Blake, I'm sure she'll soon settle in.' She didn't wait for a response; she closed the gate and walked back up the ramp to the classroom, her eyes on the little boy in front who'd provided a welcome distraction.

Chloe made a beeline for her while the children sat themselves down on the carpet. 'What did Mia's dad want?'

'Oh nothing really, he was telling me Mia's a little emotional this morning.'

'He's so cute, isn't he?' she said, a grin on her face that reminded Alex of being a teenager, gossiping with friends in the girls toilets at school.

'Is he? I hadn't noticed.'

CHAPTER FIVE

Alex opened a bottle of wine. It had been a long week. She'd managed to avoid Ryan at school by asking Chloe to go out and let the children in on Friday morning while she waited by the classroom door, hiding. It had reminded her of being a child, hovering outside her bedroom and watching as her dad returned home from a stint out at sea – always late and never sober.

Alex had been determined not to make eye contact with Ryan, focusing instead on the children as they made their way inside. She'd been watching him from the classroom through a narrow opening in the blinds, observing his obvious agitation from afar where it felt harmless. He'd been dressed for work, a pale blue shirt tucked into dark grey trousers, his work lanyard hanging around his neck. He'd held Mia's hand but his eyes had been on the door, waiting for it to open.

She'd watched his reaction as Chloe appeared and made her way down to the playground, his eyes flitting around, searching. He'd worn his disappointment so vividly that Alex had felt sure someone would see it and wonder what was wrong.

She'd felt the stirrings of something in her chest and realised that she'd been pleased; she'd *wanted* him to notice her absence. To *feel* it. Despite every part of herself knowing it was wrong, and knowing that nothing could happen, she couldn't help the raw and uncontrollable desire. It felt limitless. Unstoppable.

She poured herself a glass of Chardonnay to have with the takeout she'd ordered, relieved that she'd made it through the week. In a few more, she reasoned, this would all be a distant memory; she would move on with her life and Ryan with his. She wondered whether he would be able to salvage his marriage or whether it had already ended; were they just existing together – Ryan and Hannah – both too afraid to walk away?

Seeing Hannah at school had only exacerbated Alex's guilt. On Wednesday morning Hannah had waited to speak to her, a couple of other parents in front passing along bits of information which Alex struggled to focus on; she could see Hannah lingering behind, her blonde hair tied up in a bun. She'd asked Alex to change Mia's reading books, thanking her with a smile and telling her to have a good day. Alex had had to excuse herself from the classroom after – she was shaking. She'd rushed off to the toilet and splashed cold water on her face and stayed there until the surge of adrenaline had begun to dissipate. Had she been expecting Hannah to confront her?

She'd drunk half the bottle of wine before she heard the intercom buzz. She pressed the button to release the front door downstairs – she didn't even feel hungry anymore, her head cloudy from the Chardonnay. She left the empty glass on the kitchen worktop ready to refill. She'd ordered a pizza; she could always save it until the morning. She opened the door.

'Hey.' Ryan was stood with his hands in his pockets, a thin smile on his face. 'I've been at work. I... I was just passing and thought I'd stop by.'

They both knew that the convenience of passing by should never supersede the wrongfulness of it. He wasn't there because the opportunity had presented itself, he was there because he wanted to be. Alex didn't respond, her head filling with conflicting things to say.

'Should I go?' he asked.

The sound of footsteps echoed along the hallway. Alex turned to see a young man walking towards them wearing a baseball cap and carrying a pizza box. He stopped as he reached them and Alex suddenly felt exposed – a stranger encroaching on their space and their secrets. He held out the box and Alex took it, the smell of the pizza filling the air. 'Thanks,' she mumbled. He nodded then turned and left. Alex waited until he'd disappeared from view before speaking again, her eyes finding Ryan's.

'Fancy some pizza?' she asked. It was a bad call, and she knew it even as she said it, but there was something greater at play, something she couldn't reason with.

'Sure.' Ryan's eyes seemed to light up. She stepped to one side and, as he passed, she felt her determination from the week evaporate.

'Go straight through.' She closed the door and followed him into the living area where the lounge and kitchen blended into one. 'I'll grab some plates. I've opened a bottle of wine if you want one?'

'I'd love one, thanks. It's been a long day.'

'What do you do for work?' She felt looser, the words flowing freely. She looked at the empty glass of wine on the side and knew the impact it had already had on her. She hesitated when pouring another, weighing up the calming effect it would have on her versus the inability to make decisions with any clarity. Deciding on somewhere in the middle, she poured herself a small glass and emptied the rest of the bottle into Ryan's.

'I'm a software developer.'

Alex handed him his drink and put the pizza and a couple of plates on the coffee table. 'I'd be terrible at that, I can barely write my lesson plans on a computer.'

'Well, I'm not sure I'd make a great teacher.'

'You're great with Mia. I've seen the way she looks at you, she idolises you.'

Ryan sat on the sofa and Alex joined him, careful to keep as much space between them as possible. Something had changed in his eyes when she mentioned Mia, as though a shadow had crept in and dimmed some of the light. 'She's a great kid.'

He took a drink before placing the glass down on the coffee table. He sat forward, his forearms resting on his knees and his back hunched over. A gap had opened up between them and their shared doubts were pouring into it, expanding and fighting for space.

'I'm sorry,' he said, his voice almost a whisper. Alex didn't need to ask what for, she understood. He was fighting a battle in his own head, one she couldn't help him with. She was an observer, watching as the disquiet crept onto his face, knowing there was nothing she could do about it.

She closed her eyes and took a deep breath, fighting for some of the strength she'd maintained all week. 'Maybe you should go home.'

He turned to face her, his eyes narrowing. 'Is that what you want?'

It was the last thing she wanted. She couldn't remember ever feeling so drawn to someone, as though a force existed between them and she was powerless to resist it. She barely knew him, and yet she knew more than enough. It felt primal. Magnetic. She shook her head almost imperceptibly, her body reacting where her mind could not.

'Me neither.' He reached out and took her hand, his eyes fixed on hers. Her skin tingled at his touch. 'I'm sorry this is putting you in a difficult position, Alex. I just don't know what to do. I can't stop thinking about you.'

'I feel the same way, but that's not a good enough reason for this, is it?' It wasn't a rhetorical question, she was genuinely interested in whether he thought that whatever existed between them was enough to excuse their indiscretions. She knew it wasn't, but she was looking to be persuaded, to allow herself to fall into his arms and not question the morality of it.

He pinched the bridge of his nose and closed his eyes. When he looked back up at her, it was with a look of purpose, as though he'd come to a decision. 'I think I deserve to be happy. I'm not a bad person, Alex, I think you know that or you wouldn't have let me in tonight. Yes, I'm married, but it's not like we're happy. We haven't been in years.'

'I don't think you're a bad person, but that doesn't make this right. If you're not happy, you have options.'

'I can't leave her.'

'Why?' Alex felt a shift in the mood and was suddenly aware that they'd made the leap from the possibility of an affair to discussing him leaving his wife. 'I'm sorry, that's none of my business.'

'No, no you're right, I *should* leave her but...' He swallowed hard as though the thing he was about to say was causing him physical discomfort. 'I'm scared she'd stop me from seeing Mia. She's threatened it before. Last year, I came so close to leaving. She said that if I walked out on her then I was saying goodbye to Mia too.'

Alex stopped herself from telling him that, should it come to an acrimonious split, there were solicitors who could help him with custody arrangements. It wasn't her place. She could see in his eyes the worry he was carrying, the fear of losing precious time with his daughter etched so clearly on his face. She felt sorry for him – he seemed genuinely conflicted; genuinely scared.

'I'd made my peace with it,' he continued. 'I thought it was a small price to pay to get to see my daughter growing up. But now...' he trailed off.

Alex put her empty glass down on the table, next to the pizza that neither of them had any intention of eating. Ryan moved towards her, his hand brushing her cheek. It felt inevitable, she realised – this moment. From that first kiss in the car park to right there in her home, a week of trying to resist something that lurked in the shadows, temporarily placated but ultimately inescapable.

CHAPTER SIX

A lex didn't want him to leave but she knew he couldn't stay. At one point, just after midnight, she thought he'd fallen asleep. She'd watched as he lay next to her, his arm tucked under her pillow, his body covered by her sheets. He'd looked so peaceful, the worry and anguish a distant memory.

She'd traced her fingers along his arm, taking in the feel of his skin, the rise and fall of his muscle. He'd opened his eyes and the corners of his mouth had curved into a half-smile. He'd reached out and pulled her into him, his arm wrapped around her back and his mouth finding hers again. She could lose herself in him, she realised; in his passion and the way that he looked at her. She could lose parts of herself she hadn't realised existed. It was like an awakening. She'd been asleep all this time and now here she was, never wanting to sleep again.

'I should go.' He slipped out from under the sheets and his feet found the floor, his back to Alex. She didn't speak, she knew there was nothing she could say. He'd been trying to leave for the past hour and at almost 2am, he'd finally made the move. Neither of them wanted Hannah to find out where he'd been; it would impact them both in different ways, their lives forever affected by something they had the opportunity to hide.

Alex watched him dress, pulling on his trousers and shirt. He turned to her as he buttoned it up, his hair messy and his eyes red and heavy.

'I want to see you again,' he said.

Alex was taken aback for a moment. She'd assumed this was a one-off, something which they both needed in the heat of the moment but neither could justify repeating.

'Ryan, we can't.'

'I thought you'd say that. Look, think about it, okay? I know I can't offer you what you deserve. It would be messy and hard and unpredictable but...' he paused and sat back down on the bed, leaning over towards her. 'I think we could have a good time together. I think it could be... exceptional.'

He grinned and it took her a moment to realise he was referencing the night that they'd met, Alex sat at the bar calling her date unexceptional. She couldn't help but smile.

She reached out and brushed her fingers through his hair. 'I'm sure it could be, but that doesn't change the fact that you're married.'

'I know that. Trust me, I know that.' He rubbed his hand over his face and exhaled slowly.

'I'm sorry.' She saw how her words affected him, the pain that flashed across his face. 'I know you don't need reminding.'

'It's just... no matter how wrong this is on paper, in my heart that's not how it feels.'

Alex's throat tightened, words she wanted to say becoming trapped. She felt exactly the same way but there was something stopping her from telling him. Pride, maybe, or fear. She couldn't understand her own feelings – the strength of them. The intensity. She'd been in relationships before – one serious and a couple not-so – but she couldn't recall ever feeling the weight of wanting someone so much. It scared her.

Ryan leaned across and kissed her on her cheek. 'Think about it, okay?'

She nodded and got up, pulling on her robe and leading him out of the bedroom. He followed her back through the lounge – the wine glasses still perched on the edge of the coffee table – and to the front door.

'Here.' He passed her his mobile. 'Put your number in there, I'll text you.'

'Isn't that a little risky?' She could imagine it, Hannah checking his phone and finding a trail of messages between them. The thought filled her with dread.

'I'll have it with me while I'm at work.' He didn't need to say any more – she understood: no messages in the evenings.

She typed in her number and passed the phone back to him. He punched something into the keypad before he pocketed it – she wondered what he'd stored her in his phone as.

He rested his hand against the door and leaned down towards her, smiling. 'I'll see you Monday.' He kissed her, long and gentle, his hand holding the small of her back, then he opened the door and left her just as he'd found her – all alone.

CHAPTER SEVEN

Alex woke late, the sun already high in the sky, masked by a cover of cloud which moved quickly with the wind. She padded barefoot into the lounge and found the untouched pizza on the coffee table beside the wine glasses. She heated a couple of slices up in the microwave and sat and ate them with the news playing in the background.

She watched the grey-haired man in the suit, headlines flashing up on the screen beneath him, and tried to focus but found that she couldn't, all she could think about was the previous night; Ryan's hands on her body, his lips on hers. Her skin prickled at the memory. She finished her pizza then went for a shower – she needed to calm her thoughts and clear her mind.

It was almost noon by the time she left her apartment, her hair freshly washed and blow dried and the smell of Ryan removed from her body. She'd put on a pair of jeans and a T-shirt and grabbed her rain jacket from the coat peg by the door. The sky looked heavy and grey, the clouds promising rainfall among the flashes of watery sunlight – April showers were looming, the end of March approaching quickly.

There was one more week left at school before the Easter holidays – two whole weeks of uninterrupted time, of lazy days and, maybe, stolen moments with Ryan. She shook her head as soon as the idea came to her, trying to physically dislodge it from her mind before it settled and began to grow into something she would never be able to have.

Her car was parked at the side of the building in the little bay reserved especially for her, the empty space beside it always vacant, reflecting the other vacancies in her life – the empty space in her bed, the empty chair across the kitchen table as she ate breakfast, the plus ones she never needed.

It didn't usually bother her too much; she'd lived alone for so long that it was simply the ordinary. Every now and again something would make her reassess, to evaluate her life in the way that society called for, and she would reach out and look for something. For *someone.*

She'd joined a dating site a couple of months earlier after attending yet another one of her friend's weddings alone. It wasn't that she'd been unable to enjoy herself, it was the weight of other people's expectations and their unfiltered sympathy – the way they tilted their head to one side when asking her whether she was seeing anyone; the way her friends deliberately kept some space between themselves and their other halves, as though their closeness would only enhance Alex's perceived loneliness; the way everyone told her she absolutely, definitely *would* meet the right person, as though Alex spent her entire existence debating this very point.

Of course there were times when she wondered whether she was destined to spend her whole life alone, but there were many times when it wasn't on her radar at all. There were even times where she was able to see the benefits of being alone – the freedom it brought, the options it provided.

She got in the car and started the engine, beginning the familiar route back to her childhood home. It hadn't escaped her that she would be driving closer to Ryan and to the home he shared with his wife and child, but she didn't think there was much chance of seeing him. She visited her parents' house most Saturdays – sometimes it was a quick coffee and a catch-up with her mum, other times it was a long walk around the woodland – but she could never recall seeing Ryan or his family while she was there.

Elwood was a small community with a lot of land; in fact, there wasn't much there *but* the land. The school where Alex worked had just shy of ninety pupils enrolled. There was a local shop, a church and a woodland with a little stream running through it. The rest was green fields and residential housing. The bus stop at the junction of Church Street and Field Street had a bus which may or may not come on the hour between ten and two, taking those that had the patience to wait to the local town.

Alex turned left at the church and followed Field Street past the school on the right and the shop on the left until she came to a little turn off for Beck Lane – if you didn't know Elwood, you probably wouldn't even notice it was there. It wasn't a road, just a potholed path barely wide enough for one car. It was flanked on either side by trees which seemed to reach out towards each other, their limbs touching to create a haphazard tunnel. A flock of birds took to the sky as she turned in, disturbed by the sound of tyres crunching against gravel.

The houses were few and far between on the lane, scattered at irregular intervals and separated by fields. The treetops were visible in the distance, their trunks coming into view as Alex took the arc in the road. Her parents' house stood to the right of the woodland, a long stony path leading to an old farmhouse. It had never been a working farm while Alex had lived there. Her mum had inherited the house from her dad who'd run the family business into the ground with his penchant for too much alcohol and not enough hard work.

The car jerked and bumped as she turned into the driveway, a cloud of dust and grit scattering up from beneath her tyres and settling on her windscreen. The old house sat back behind an overgrown garden, small and neglected. As Alex parked her car, she saw that the paint was peeling on the old shutter-style windows, and that the ivy at the front and side of the house was taking over, fighting for more space.

Her dad did a shoddy job of maintaining the property. He'd been a seafarer a long time ago – he would be gone for a month at a time, then home for a few weeks. His return to the family home always unsettled the peace; he'd come back tired and grumpy and – Alex always thought – desperate to get back on the water.

He'd given up trying to make amends for the years he'd neglected them. Alex told herself she was past the point of caring, and she tried to manifest that as a reality, yet she couldn't help feeling betrayed. She'd spent her childhood telling herself that he simply didn't have the time to be the man that he wanted to be – the *father* he wanted to be – and now, here he was with all the time that he never had, and he had retreated further and further into the shadows of the old house he existed in. He was no longer at sea, but he was no more present than if he were; he was suspended somewhere in between, his physical being there in the house, his heart and soul left out on the ocean.

As Alex contemplated her father's shortcomings, she felt a lump forming in her throat. Here she was, two feet on the floor walking towards her childhood home, and yet her heart was elsewhere, aching for a man who'd betrayed his family.

CHAPTER EIGHT

Alex's mum opened the door wearing a floral apron, her hands covered in flour and her glasses perched on top of her head.

'Hello, dear.' Carol smiled. 'Good timing, I've just put a cake in the oven.'

Alex could smell the sweetness of chocolate as soon as she stepped inside. She breathed it in. It always felt nostalgic when her mum baked; she could remember helping her as a little girl, a wooden spoon in her hand which she couldn't wait to lick clean and a stool beneath her feet. They would often bake while her dad was away and, as the years passed, Alex came to realise it was a hobby reserved strictly for those times. She wasn't sure whether her mum was celebrating his absence or whether she simply did not have the mental fortitude for it while he was home. Alex never asked.

'Smells delicious.'

'Chocolate orange,' she said, leading Alex into the kitchen and filling up the kettle. 'Tea?'

'Yes, please. Dad home?'

'He's in bed,' she said, and Alex didn't ask why. Her dad often slept during the day and woke at night. He said it was the consequence of a life out at sea and the lack of routine, but Alex couldn't help wondering if it was because he preferred the quiet of the night.

'Have you had a good week?' Alex asked.

'Yes, I've been busy actually. I've joined a walking group.' Carol smiled brightly and Alex was reminded of being in class, when one of the children had done something they were particularly proud of. It warmed Alex's heart.

'Mum that's great! Tell me about it.'

'It's only a small group, half a dozen or so. We meet at the entrance to the woodland and walk a few miles before going to the church for refreshments. They open up every Wednesday and Friday, you know?'

'No I didn't know that, but it sounds wonderful!'

'I must say, I quite enjoyed myself. I went to both groups and met some lovely folk – did you know Margaret Larwood's moved into a care home?' She didn't give Alex chance to answer. 'A lovely couple have moved into her bungalow – Edward and Rosemary. They've moved here from down south, said they could get a lot more for their money... anyway, they've started the group and Nancy comes along too and Elaine and Jerry.'

Alex sat back in her chair and smiled as her mum pottered around the kitchen making tea and checking on the cake. It was the happiest Alex had heard her sound in a while. Her mum had long since shied away from the community she'd grown up in and Alex was never quite sure why, though she had her suspicions. She thought it must have something to do with her dad – maybe he'd had an affair with someone in the village or caused a scene when he was drunk one night at the local pub, something which had caused her mum to retreat into the old house and hide herself away, embarrassed of a husband who repeatedly let her down.

'Here you go, dear.' She passed Alex a mug of tea and sat down across the table from her. 'How's school?'

'Good, thanks. Looking forward to the holidays though.'

'Anything nice planned?'

Alex shrugged and took a sip of her tea, her mind flitting to Ryan.

'Oh, I know that face,' she teased. 'Who's the lucky man?'

'No, there's no man.'

'I'm your mum, Alexandra, I know when my little girl's smitten. I could tell when it was Jay Weaver and you were thirteen, I could tell when it was Robert Styles at comprehensive, and I can tell just as easily now.'

A timer went off from the kitchen worktop; her mum got up and slipped her hands into a pair of yellow oven gloves. Steam billowed from the oven as she opened it and she stepped back for a second before her hands disappeared inside, returning with a round metal tin. She placed it on the counter and prodded at it with a cake tester. 'Perfect.' She returned to the oven and pulled another identical tin out, placing it on the counter alongside the first. 'We can have some once it's cooled. Now where were we? Oh yes, you were about to tell me about this new man of yours.'

Alex thought for a moment, torn between wanting to tell her mum everything and knowing that she wouldn't approve. She didn't want to disappoint her. Somewhere amid the jumbling thoughts in her mind she decided on a half-truth. 'It's... complicated. He's not always available.' Her mum raised her eyebrows. 'Work...' she lied.

'Ah, I see. He's a busy man?'

'Yes, he certainly is.'

'You know, I understand a thing or two about that.' There was a sadness in her eyes that spoke of a pain she usually tried to hide from Alex and it made her regret mentioning anything. 'Men who apply all their focus elsewhere can be very difficult to coexist with. It's easy to romanticise it as some great love story but, sadly, it's often without the happy ending.'

It was as though Alex was watching her mother for the first time through a completely different pair of eyes. She saw her as a young woman, in love with a man she hadn't yet realised was married to the ocean, a man who she chose to see as an old romantic, returning after weeks away, hungry for her. She could see her as a friend, her worries about the time he would be gone placated by the strength he brought with him on his return; her concerns about whether they would stand the test of time and distance conciliated by the old notion of 'absence makes the heart grow fonder'. Except it hadn't, and instead their love had weakened – rotted – and grown into something else; something ugly but permanent, fixed by – Alex worried – herself.

'Mum,' Alex said softly. 'It's never too late, you know.'

Her mum exhaled then tried to laugh but it quickly petered out. 'Oh, Alex, your dad and I have our troubles but we've been married for a long time. But you… you're still young. There are so many men that would feel lucky to be with you.' Carol reached out and patted Alex's hand. 'You don't need to feel as though you're trying to make yourself fit into someone else's life – it gets very uncomfortable.'

As though on cue, the noise of footsteps could be heard from upstairs, followed by a door shutting. They finished their tea in silence, listening, until they heard the hissing of the toilet flushing followed by footsteps padding back into the bedroom above them.

'Why don't we go out for a walk while the cake cools?' Alex suggested.

'Yes, let's.'

CHAPTER NINE

The ground was wet from the rain that had swept through with haste. Translucent sunlight fell in through the canopy of trees and scattered among the forest floor. Alex could just make out fractured pieces of blue sky, the clouds clearing after the downpour. She breathed in the smell of the woodland she knew so well, the earthy scents so vividly nostalgic.

She could remember playing on a rope swing as a child; she could have been no older than eleven or twelve. The neighbourhood kids were taking it in turns to hurtle over the stream, steep banks slippery from the April showers.

She could remember her feet leaving the ground followed by a loud crack. For a moment she thought it was thunder, but she quickly realised from the slack in the rope that it was the sound of the tree branch breaking overhead. The rope was still clutched in her hands as she hit the ground, landing awkwardly on her ankle and falling into the stream. It wasn't deep but it was cold, and it was this she still remembered – the shock of the water as it soaked her clothes and took her breath. That and the embarrassment.

'We're bringing the children here after Easter for a school

trip.'

'To the local woods? Don't you usually take them to Chatsworth House or Twycross Zoo?'

'Yes, we'll be doing something like that in the summer, but we're learning about habitats next term so I thought we'd do a little scavenger hunt, look for insects, that kind of thing.'

'I'm sure they'll enjoy that. You spent hours here as a child, you used to love it.'

'I still do.'

They skirted the edge of the stream before following the path which led into the middle of the woodland. The sound of the current followed them for a while; there'd been a lot of rain and the water level had begun to rise, swelling at the banks, but eventually it was replaced by the whispering of the wind through the undergrowth.

'We came through this way on Wednesday with the group,' her mum said, gesturing to the path in front of them. 'Edward and Rosemary couldn't say enough nice things about the place. It seemed funny really, seeing somewhere you know so well through a fresh pair of eyes. It reminded me how lucky we are and how much I've taken it for granted.'

'I'm so pleased you've found a group you enjoy. Carry on going, won't you?'

Her mum looked at her questioningly at first as though she didn't understand what she meant, but then her face softened and she smiled weakly, an understanding passing between them – *Don't let Dad make you stop doing something you enjoy.*

'You don't need to worry about me, Alexandra, I'm okay.'

The path narrowed, overgrown grass reaching out and dampening Alex's jeans as she walked in single file behind her mum, the path no longer wide enough to accommodate them side by side. Birdsong filled the silence that had settled between them, accompanied by the crunch of their footsteps against the gravelly path and the occasional flutter of the leaves as the wind disturbed the trees. By the time the path broadened again the songs of the birds had been replaced by the sounds of laughter and the unmistakeable squeals of children playing.

They approached a grassy clearing in the heart of the woods where a couple of picnic tables had been placed by the neighbourhood committee. Trees encircled it, wildflowers shooting up among the grass. It had always felt like a secret garden to Alex, hidden away in the middle of an enchanted land. It had been one of her favourite spots as a child – though the picnic benches weren't there back then. She would lie on the long grass and watch the circle of sky visible above, looking for planes or birds or clouds shaped like all the weird and wonderful things which filled a child's mind.

The sound of the children's laughter carried through the enclosure of trees as they approached it. Alex smiled; the innocence of children was what had drawn her to teaching, their ability to turn the mundane into something magical. Seeing the world through their eyes felt like a fairy tale, as though she were reliving her own childhood time and time again. When the stresses of the job got to her, it was the children she listened to in order to remind her why she was there.

Alex and Carol weaved their way between a patch of silver birch trees, flashes of colour visible on the other side. Sat on one of the picnic benches were two women and two men, all facing each other, and stood beside them were another man and woman, their backs to the rest as they watched something in one of the surrounding trees.

Their voices were lost among the chaos of the four children who were running around them, squealing and laughing in delight. It was one of the children who recognised Alex first – she was used to it, whenever she came to her childhood home and walked the familiar paths of the woodland she would inevitably see someone she knew.

'Miss Vaughn!' came a voice, high-pitched and full of

excitement. The girl ran towards her, her blonde hair flowing over her shoulders and her cheeks flushed pink. 'Look! Look what I found!'

Alex felt hot despite the cool winds; her legs felt weak and hands clammy. She tried to smile but her body no longer felt under her command. The other children joined Mia who stood in front of Alex with her arm outstretched, a snail in the palm of her hand.

'This is my teacher!' Mia exclaimed.

'Mia! A snail… wow! Fantastic!' Alex used all the enthusiasm she could muster, a smile fixed to her face which felt uncomfortable, her cheeks aching under the pressure.

'Carol!' One of the women who'd been sat at the picnic table was walking towards them, approaching Alex's mum.

'Rosemary, hi!' Alex's mum gestured towards her. 'This is my daughter, Alexandra. Alexandra this is Rosemary and the gentleman over there is Edward, I was telling you about them earlier, remember? From my walking group?'

'Yes, of course. Nice to meet you.' Alex waved over in Edward's direction and as she did so she saw Ryan sat opposite him, Hannah by his side. He looked at her and smiled and Alex felt herself redden, the heat swelling across her chest.

Hannah got up from the bench and walked over to Mia, looking at Alex. 'Hi, Miss Vaughn. We've been out exploring, haven't we, Mia? She's so excited about the nature walk you have planned after the holidays.'

'I'm glad to hear it! You'll be able to help me, won't you, Mia?'

Mia giggled and one of the other children pulled her away to an area they'd transformed into an obstacle course; logs and rocks acting as makeshift jumps and stepping stones.

'My son is here for the weekend,' Rosemary told them, pointing over to the man stood beside the bench. 'Ben, and that's his wife Penny, and our grandchildren…' She tried to point to the children as they jumped around. 'Theo, Oscar and Minnie.'

'How lovely.' Carol smiled. 'They certainly seem to be enjoying themselves.'

'We've just been telling Ryan and Hannah that we're having a barbeque tonight – they've agreed to come. I saw Nancy earlier and asked her too. A bit of a late house warming, really. Why don't you join us?' She directed the question to Carol, and Alex was momentarily relieved. She felt herself taking a step backwards, trying to hide away in the shadow of the trees.

'Oh that sounds lovely, but Terry isn't feeling well...'

'Why don't you come with Alexandra?'

Alex saw Ryan turn to face them, but she couldn't see his expression – was he panicking like she was?

'That's a good idea. You haven't got anything on, have you?' Alex's mum had turned to face her, her eyes full of expectation and excitement. They hadn't done anything like that together in a long time and, in any other circumstances, Alex would be excited about it too. But this... No, she couldn't. She knew it was a bad idea and yet she couldn't find an excuse quickly enough. The silence stretched out and she could feel Rosemary and Hannah's eyes on her, waiting.

'I don't want to intrude...' she tried, hoping her mum would take the hint.

'Not at all, the more the merrier! See you about six?'

Alex smiled, it was all she could do.

Hannah was still stood opposite her, her blonde hair loose and wavy, a black headband pushing it back from her face. 'We'll see you later, then!'

'Yes, see you later.'

Alex couldn't be sure – she was tired and felt suffocated by the circumstances – but she thought she'd seen Hannah's eyes flit straight to Ryan, as though she'd been looking for a reaction. Alex took a deep breath, trying to let the thought wash away, but it didn't: it seemed to stick, clinging on and demanding her attention.

CHAPTER TEN

A lex had managed to persuade her mum to cut their walk short so she'd have time to go home and change before the barbecue. She quickly ate a piece of the cake that had cooled to placate her mum, before jumping into her car and driving home, her head mentally sorting through the outfits in her wardrobe. She wanted to look nice without looking like she'd *tried* to look nice.

Once she was home she had a quick shower, straightened her hair, then rifled through her clothes, settling on a teal green midi dress, denim jacket and white trainers. She wore make-up, but not too much, and a couple of sprays of her favourite perfume.

By the time Alex got back to her parents' house it was 5:55. Her mum greeted her at the door in a pair of jeans and a white linen blouse. She looked nice – her greying hair curled under at the ends and a glossy pink sheen on her lips.

'You look lovely, Mum.'

'Thanks, dear, so do you. Look at us, girls' night out!'

They got in the car and Alex drove the short distance to Edward and Rosemary's place, a large bungalow on Hayfield Road, a long curved street opposite the school. She parked outside and checked her reflection quickly in the mirror. She still looked tired, dark circles under her eyes that she'd tried to disguise with concealer.

The bungalow was set back from the street behind a large garden with neatly tended borders and a long driveway running down the side of the property. They could hear noise coming from the back, children playing and music on low. Her mum took the lead, walking to the metal gate at the back and letting herself through.

'Carol, you made it!' Edward walked towards her and embraced her gently. He was a large man with kind eyes and a thick mane of grey hair, his eyebrows equally as wild and untamed. He was wearing a thin blue jumper and a pair of jeans. 'Can I get you both a drink?'

'Yes please, wine would be lovely.'

'Red or white?'

'I think I'll go for a red.'

'Alexandra? Wine?'

'No thank you, Edward, I'm driving.'

'Tea, coffee, juice, water?'

'Just some water would be great, thanks.' Alex's eyes skirted the garden. It was a large open space with a shed at the bottom and hedges lining the boundary. The lawn was neatly mowed and the patio area spotless, rattan furniture covering most of it with a large glass-topped table in the centre. Patio doors at the back of the property led into a large kitchen diner. She didn't spot Ryan straight away, nor Hannah and Mia, but as she sat down they all came walking out from the bungalow accompanied by Rosemary.

'Carol, hi! I've just been giving a tour. Do you want to come and have a look around?'

'I would love to!' Carol followed Rosemary into the bungalow and, on her way, Edward passed her a glass of wine. Alex wondered whether she should have got up and followed, but she didn't have much interest in taking a tour of a stranger's house –

she'd never understood what made people offer to give them as though it were some kind of prize for being invited round. Alex had never offered to give anyone a tour of her flat – not that there was much to see. Edward passed her a glass of water as Mia came running over.

'Miss Vaughn, you look pretty!'

'Oh that's very kind of you, Mia. And look at you! You look like a princess!' She was wearing a pink dress with a white cardigan and a floral headband in her hair.

'Hello.' Hannah sat beside her and Ryan took the next seat along, Hannah a barrier between them in more ways than one. Ryan didn't look awkward or embarrassed; she wondered whether it was taking a lot of effort on his part, as it was her, or whether it came naturally to him. Her forced casualness was causing her to question her every move – did she usually cross her legs? Fold her arms? Would she usually sit with a smile on her face or keep her expression neutral?

She couldn't help imagining Ryan's mouth on hers; the way his hands had held her hips the previous night; the way she'd moaned in his ear. She felt the stirring of longing deep inside her. She bit her lip absentmindedly and, as she caught Ryan's eye, she saw him grinning at her, his eyes holding hers for a moment longer than she felt he should have.

'You've met my husband, Ryan, haven't you?' Hannah gestured flippantly beside her.

'Yes, briefly at school.' Alex immediately regretted her words. She felt silly for adding *at school*, as though Hannah would think this were an odd statement to make. But if she did, she didn't show it.

'Hello, Mia's told me a lot about you.' Ryan smiled. He had a bottle of Budweiser in his hand and Alex saw that he'd changed. He was wearing a denim shirt with a pair of cream chinos. He looked nice. *Too nice.* It made her feel uncomfortable, her desire too hard to swallow. She felt sure someone would notice.

'She's a delight to have in the class.'

'She can be a little terror at home at the minute.' Hannah laughed but Mia looked mortified.

'Mummy!' she moaned.

'It's true!'

'She's an angel at school. Very helpful and eager to learn. You can't be good all the time, I suppose!' Alex tried not to look at Ryan but she didn't particularly want to make eye contact with Hannah either. She felt sure Hannah would see something in her eyes, the lies and the betrayal.

'That's what I always say; if it's a choice, I would rather she behaved at school.' Ryan took a long drink of his beer.

'Easy for you to say, you're not the one who has to deal with it.' Hannah laughed again but it wasn't genuine – it was a well-placed laugh to disguise the resentment so clear in her words.

Alex stole a glance at Ryan who had clenched his mouth shut, his fingers turning the bottle in his hands. Mia ran off to play with the other children and Alex watched her go, taking note of the other people who were chatting in the garden. She recognised a couple – Nancy, her mum's friend from the village who Alex hadn't seen in years; Wendy and Neil who owned the local village store; a couple of parents of children Alex had taught a few years earlier.

'It's nice to hear she's so well behaved at school.' Hannah had a glass of wine in her hand and she took a long drink from it, almost draining the contents.

Alex could feel Ryan's eyes on her. She tried to avoid looking at him but, while Hannah was distracted watching Mia play, she gave in, looking over to him and raising her eyebrows. He moved his eyes deliberately from her to the house a couple of times then stood. 'I'm going to go and get another drink, Han. Do you want one?'

Hannah responded by finishing the rest of her wine then holding the empty glass in an outstretched arm. Ryan took it from her but Hannah didn't even turn towards him; she had the slightly glazed expression of someone who'd had more than a couple of drinks already.

Alex watched Ryan walk away. When he got to the kitchen he looked back over his shoulder. Was he asking her to follow him? Without letting herself think about it, caught in her longing to be near him, she cleared her throat then stood up. 'I'm going to go and see if I can find my mum and pop to the toilet.'

Hannah smiled. 'Okay.'

Alex stepped through the patio doors into a large rectangular room with exposed brick at either end, the other two walls painted a dark shade of blue. A row of lights hung low over a large wooden island and a huge vase of sunflowers sat on top of it. She wondered whether it had been like this when Mrs Larwood had lived here – she suspected not.

Edward was busy separating sausages ready for the barbecue and Alex's mum and Rosemary were nowhere to be seen. Alex recognised Ben, their son, and his wife stood talking to another couple in the kitchen, and a few of the children were watching something on the television hung on the far wall. Alex slipped past them all and walked quickly through to the hallway.

The front door stood at the end of a well-lit pale green corridor, pictures adorning the walls and two wooden doors on either side. She wasn't sure what to do, whether to retreat back into the kitchen or try one of the rooms leading off the hall, hoping to find a toilet or her mum and Rosemary – or maybe Ryan. Before she'd made up her mind, one of the doors on the right opened and Ryan's hand grabbed her forearm, pulling her inside. She almost squealed, the movement so quick it took her by surprise.

Ryan closed the door and locked it. 'Fancy seeing you here,' he whispered.

'Ryan, we can't... not here...' but her protestations disappeared the moment his mouth found hers, kissing her slowly at first and then with greed. His hands slipped around her waist then lifted her up off the floor, pressing her back into the wall. She wrapped her legs around him, her dress hitched above her knees. She'd never felt passion like this; she'd never *needed* someone the way she felt she needed Ryan.

After a couple of minutes they heard voices outside – they stopped kissing abruptly and could just make out Rosemary telling Carol about the renovations they'd had done. Their voices trailed away as they disappeared back into the kitchen. Ryan let go of his hold on Alex and her feet reluctantly found the tiled floor. She didn't want him to let go. She didn't want the moment to end at all. She pulled him back into her, her hands grasping at his shirt, fumbling with the buttons. He took her hands in his, stopping her.

'I'll come round later.' His voice was low and breathless, his hair ruffled.

'Tonight?'

'Yeah, that okay?'

'What about…' Alex looked to her right, in the direction of the garden and his family. She didn't want to say their names.

'Don't worry. I'll see you later, okay?'

She nodded. 'I'll go first, you need to sort your hair out.'

He smiled playfully then lent towards the door to unlock it, kissing her briefly as he did. She slipped out into the hallway and was relieved to find she was alone. She readjusted her dress, ran her fingers through her hair, then took a deep breath and walked back into the kitchen.

'There you are!' Her mum was stood at the island with an empty glass of wine in her hand. Edward was undoing another bottle as the unmistakeable smell of the barbecue wafted into the house. The light was fading outside, a slither of a crescent moon visible between the patches of cloud. The rain had held off, the evening turning into a mild one for the time of year.

Alex smiled. 'Just popped to the toilet.'

'Rosemary's been showing me around, it's lovely, isn't it?' Carol said.

Alex nodded. 'Yes, I was just admiring the decor.'

Edward uncorked the wine. 'Thank you, it's all Rosemary's doing really, but while she's not here I suppose I could take the credit!'

'I love what you've done with the place!' Ryan appeared behind Alex and swept past without acknowledging her. 'I've just been looking at your reading room. Great choice of books!' He helped himself to a bottle of beer from the fridge then poured another glass of wine for Hannah.

'Thank you! Feel free to borrow any. Rosemary is always telling me I have far too many. This is Carol Vaughn and her daughter Alexandra, have you met?'

'Miss Vaughn is Mia's teacher, but I haven't met *Mrs* Vaughn before.' He held out his hand to Carol and she shook it, smiling broadly. 'Nice to meet you.'

'And you.'

Ryan took the drinks and disappeared back outside, his hair still slightly less groomed than it had been.

Alex spent the rest of the evening trying to blend into the small crowds, sticking with her mum where possible and avoiding Ryan and Hannah. Just after nine, she suggested they'd better be going and her mum agreed – she'd had three glasses of wine and her cheeks were flushed pink. They said their goodbyes to Edward and Rosemary and slipped through the gate at the back without having to see Ryan and Hannah again. Part of Alex felt rude; under normal circumstances she would have sought them out and politely said goodbye. But she couldn't bring herself to – it felt contrived and twisted and… wrong.

She drove her mum back to the house, the sporadically lit Beck Lane notoriously difficult to navigate without the daylight. Carol asked her if she wanted to stay the night but she declined, telling her she needed to be up early to meet a friend. They said their goodbyes and Alex turned the car around, watching her mum through the rear-view mirror as she stood waving in the dimly lit entrance to the house.

Alex headed back down Beck Lane and through the residential streets of Elwood, leaving the small village behind as she drove towards Nottingham. She wanted to get home and tidy up, maybe even change her sheets and take another shower. She put the radio on and listened to the music on low as she joined the bypass.

Despite knowing it was wrong; despite it going against the moral code she'd always abided by; despite knowing the dangers involved, she was excited – *desperate* even – to be alone with Ryan again, to have him to herself physically in a way she knew she couldn't emotionally.

As she pulled into her parking space beside the apartment block, her phone vibrated in her bag; she reached over and grabbed it to find a message from a number she didn't recognise.

> Be there in an hour.

She added the number to her contacts – first using his name then changing her mind and simply storing it under the letter *R* – then got out of the car. The street was quiet, the only noise coming from the steady flow of traffic on the main road nearby. A couple of lights were on in the other apartments, and she could see the glow of the TV in a ground-floor window. As she was fumbling around trying to unlock the front door, she heard a sudden noise. It sounded closer than the road, and different.

Startled, she dropped her keys, the metal clanging against the pavement. She turned to look behind her, her eyes darting left and right. She listened, wondering what exactly it was that she'd heard. It was a cross between a gasp and a cry, as though someone had tripped or fallen and tried to stifle their response.

She waited, not daring to bend down and retrieve her keys

until she was satisfied that no one was lurking in the shadows. She could hear cars speeding past and, somewhere nearby, a door shutting. Alex bent to pick up her keys and unlocked the door, her heart racing as she rushed to get inside. She couldn't work out why it had unnerved her so much.

She closed the door behind her and rested her back against it, trying to catch her breath, and as she did she heard the unmistakeable sound of a car engine revving, tyres spinning against the road as it sped away. She peered out of the narrow strip of glass in the door and saw a dark-coloured hatchback heading towards the main road, barely stopping before pulling out into the intermittent traffic.

She swallowed down a bitter taste in her mouth, telling herself she was just being paranoid – there were loads of cars that particular style and colour on the roads, it didn't mean anything that it happened to be the same as the one she'd seen just over a week before, leaving the estate behind Ryan.

CHAPTER ELEVEN

R yan arrived just before eleven. Alex had changed three times – from her dress to some lingerie, back to her dress and then into the lingerie with a long black robe over the top. She'd applied coconut body butter and sprayed her favourite perfume. She'd lit a candle in the bedroom then blown it out – she didn't want him to think she was trying to romanticise the situation.

Then she'd sat on the sofa and waited, absentmindedly flicking through her phone, waiting to see whether he would text her again to say he couldn't make it. Every now and again she'd parted the curtains and looked outside into the night hoping to see a set of headlights approaching, only to be disappointed when met with nothing but a blanket of stars above the rooftops.

Time had passed slowly. She couldn't help thinking about the car she'd seen driving away from the estate – the way it had left in a hurry and how similar it had been to the car that had followed Ryan's over a week earlier. She'd kept telling herself it was the stress of the situation – she wasn't used to lying – but there was an uncomfortable niggling feeling which had refused to relent. She'd stood and began pacing the room, trying to burn off the paranoia.

When he arrived he'd text her from outside. *Here.* She pressed the buzzer to release the front door downstairs then waited until she heard footsteps out in the hallway. She opened the door but neither of them spoke. His eyes travelled up and down her body before he took her in his arms and kissed her hard. He carried her into the bedroom and undressed her slowly, taking his time, less haste than the night before. It was different, less rushed yet somehow more urgent.

At some point in the early hours of the morning, a cool breeze blowing in from the open window, Ryan turned to her. 'I don't want to go,' he whispered, his breath warm against her cheek.

Alex wanted to tell him to stay, but she knew it was futile. Instead, she reached out and traced her finger up and down the smooth contour of the muscle in his arm.

'Your mum seems nice.'

The change in conversation surprised her. She stopped what she was doing and looked at him. 'Yes, she is.'

'You're close?'

'Yes, I see her most weekends.'

'What about your dad?'

Alex lay back and looked at the ceiling. She didn't want thoughts of her dad to taint the moment, to pop the bubble she was existing in with the sharpness of his failures.

'Sorry, I was just curious.'

'No, don't be sorry. We've never been close. Mum and Dad are still together but... he's a complicated man.' Alex hoped that would be enough to put Ryan off asking anything more, but she could tell by the way he moved closer to her and propped his head up on his hand that it wasn't.

'Complicated?'

'Yeah... he was a seafarer so he was away a lot. And when he came back it was as though not all of him did. Each time, it was like he left another piece of himself behind.'

'What does he do now?'

'Nothing. Just wallows in bed most of the time. It's as though his life has been one giant disappointment.'

'I'm sure that's more about him than it is you or your mum, but then I bet you know that already.'

'Yes. No. Sometimes.' Alex carried on staring at the ceiling, Ryan's hand resting on her bare stomach. She couldn't believe how freely the words were flowing; how much she felt able to open up. It wasn't something she usually did. Somehow, over the years, the way her dad behaved had come to feel like a reflection on her, as though people would judge her through association. It was the same way her mum felt, Alex suspected. But lying there with Ryan, she didn't feel that way at all.

'I never knew my dad.' Ryan moved his mouth closer to her and kissed her shoulder tenderly.

'I'm sorry. That can't have been easy.'

'I'm close to my mum. Having one good parent is a lot more than some people.'

'Does she live around here?'

'Not far – Sheffield. She lives on the same street as my sister, not far from where I grew up.'

'You have a sister?'

'Yeah, Leanne.'

'I always wanted a sister.'

He laughed. 'You can have her, she's a pain in the arse.'

Alex couldn't help but relish the ordinary conversation, unremarkable yet, to her, a pleasant surprise. She felt as though she knew him a little better for it – was his own lack of a father figure the reason he was so against leaving Hannah?

'Where did you say you were going tonight?' She'd had to rephrase the question in her mind a few times before she asked it.

She didn't want to say *'Where did you tell Hannah you were going?'* or *'Where does your wife think you are?'*

'For a few drinks with friends.'

Despite her careful wording, Alex noticed his voice change slightly as he spoke, tinged by the weight of shame. She turned back onto her side so she was almost nose to nose with him. The only light came from the milky glow of the moon filtering in through the open window; the only sound from the occasional car passing on the main road beyond the estate.

She tried to see him properly in the dark, to take in his features – the remarkable blue eyes, the dimples in his cheeks, the way his smile started on one side slightly before the other. She rested her palm on the side of his face and felt the beginnings of stubble beneath his skin.

Alex wanted to ask him when she would see him again but held back the words she feared would make her sound needy. She didn't want to risk scaring him away.

It was Ryan who spoke next, his voice low, his hand resting on her hip beneath the sheets. 'What have you got planned this week?'

She didn't have any plans. Sometimes, on Wednesdays, she met her friend Emma for food in Nottingham, but that had become less frequent lately since Emma had started seeing Owen, a guy she'd met online just before Christmas. The last time Alex had seen her was almost six weeks earlier and Emma had droned on and on about whether Owen's friendship with an ex-girlfriend was a red flag or whether she was just being sensitive.

Alex had tried to play the role of supportive friend but there was only so much she could take. Emma was an independent, intelligent woman, and it had pained Alex to see her shedding tears in the middle of a restaurant over a man who insisted he still see his ex-girlfriend. Emma wasn't looking for advice, or at least not the honest type Alex had tried to offer.

Other than the occasional midweek meet up with Emma, Alex didn't venture out a lot in the evenings – she was a morning person. She liked the early hours when everything was quiet and still, before most people were awake and the chaos began. Evenings, for her, tended to be about preparing for the next day then winding down with a Netflix series and a glass of wine.

'Not a lot, it'll be a mad week at work before breaking up on Friday.'

'So if I was able to come round Tuesday after work, you'd be home?'

'Yes, I'll be home.' Part of her had considered telling him she wasn't sure – she didn't want to seem too available, content to wait around for him to reappear. But she was also mindful of wanting to make it easy for him to come to her.

He held her close to him, his arms wrapped around her shoulders and her cheek pressed against his chest. She could hear his heart beating, strong and steady. He kissed the top of her head and she knew that he was trying to find the willpower to leave.

When he let his grip on her go she didn't wait for him to speak; she rolled over and grabbed her robe from the shaggy rug beside her bed, slipping the robe on and opening the door. She left him to dress while she got a drink of water from the kitchen and, as she stood resting against the worktop, she noticed the clock on the wall showing almost 2am.

Ryan joined her a couple of minutes later, his denim shirt half buttoned, his trousers creased from being screwed up on the floor. She hoped Hannah would be asleep when he got home so she wouldn't see him like this, dishevelled and bleary-eyed. Alex put her glass down on the kitchen worktop and watched as he slipped on his trainers.

'I'll see you Monday...' he said, then reading Alex's confused expression he clarified: 'At school.'

'Oh, yes.' She didn't want to think about work because

thinking about it caused a wave of guilt so intense it seemed to twist her insides.

She joined him at the door and he kissed her gently, one hand brushing her cheek while the other held on to her back. He didn't say goodbye, he simply stepped out into the hallway and turned left. She stood watching as he walked to the end of the corridor and disappeared down the stairs, then she closed the door and stifled a yawn. She was exhausted.

Back in her bedroom she closed the window and straightened up the bed before getting under the covers, the smell of Ryan lingering, the memories of the last few hours ingrained in her mind. Sleep came easily, propelled by exhaustion both physical and emotional, images of Ryan swimming in her mind as though from underwater, blurred but beautiful.

She wanted to reach out and touch him but, as her arm groggily found the empty place beside her, she realised she couldn't. She would have to be content with her memories, the empty spaces seeming suddenly bigger than ever.

CHAPTER TWELVE

Monday came and went in a haze. Alex had spent all day on Sunday feeling as though she were in a dream, living a life that wasn't hers. The early stirrings of what she knew could easily be love were met by the harsh reality of knowing he was married. Unobtainable. She knew he had no intentions of leaving Hannah and Mia, and yet, somewhere in the shadowy parts of her mind, she couldn't help but imagine him changing his mind. In these daydreams their love was insurmountable. Nothing could stop them.

Ryan had dropped Mia off at school while Alex was answering a flurry of questions about the school clubs over the Easter holidays. She noticed him try to hold back, to linger behind the other parents, but Mia had spotted her friend near the front and slipped into the classroom with her. He'd smiled as he left, at Mia and at Alex, but there had been no opportunity to talk.

By Tuesday evening Alex felt as though a weight had settled on her chest and slowly eased its way inside her, occupying her lungs and making it difficult for her to breathe. Was this how it would be, falling for a man like Ryan? Would she always feel as though she was waiting for stolen moments, never knowing for sure they would arrive? She looked at the clock on the wall – it was almost seven. She tried to recall his words from Saturday: '*So if I was able to come round Tuesday after work, you'd be home?*'

She'd had a shower and decided to sit watching repeats of *Friends* on Netflix to pass the time with a glass of wine and a share-size bar of Galaxy caramel – she hadn't been able to eat properly all day, her lunch remaining in the fridge in the staffroom and her dinner never having made it out of the freezer. It felt like torture, waiting for a man who may or may not turn up, hoping that he would and knowing the impact it would have if he didn't.

Halfway through the third episode of *Friends* her phone vibrated on the sofa beside her.

I'm here.

She felt the weight in her chest freefall, it was as though she could breathe properly again. She turned off the TV and walked over to the door, buzzing the intercom to let him in downstairs.

A minute later she heard footsteps in the hallway. She opened the door to see him hurrying towards her. A smile broke onto his face which reflected hers and in the briefest of moments he'd swept her up into his arms, her feet leaving the floor with ease. He carried her inside and kicked the door shut behind him.

'I'm sorry, I got here as soon as I could.' He lowered her to the ground and took a step back as though looking at her properly for the first time. 'Sometimes I...' He rubbed a hand over his mouth as though debating whether to carry on. Eventually, he did. 'I forget how beautiful you are.' There was such sincerity in his eyes, a seriousness that seemed to sharpen his features. She could feel her cheeks blushing, heat spreading down her neck.

'Stop!' She laughed.

'I mean it.' He took her hand and pulled her back towards him. 'I'm glad I'm here.'

'I'm glad you're here too.'

'Did you save me some?' He looked over to the slab of chocolate, which sat on the coffee table next to her empty glass.

'I'm not sure I'm ready to share my chocolate with you yet.'

'Maybe you could make an exception, I haven't eaten.'

'All day?'

'I had breakfast but I've been so busy, I haven't had chance.'

'You must be starving. I haven't had any dinner either, actually.' They looked at each other and something passed between them, an acknowledgement that they couldn't go out to eat together like a normal couple would. 'I would offer to cook but I don't think you deserve such cruelty.'

'Shall we order?'

It was strange – it was just a food order yet Alex felt like there was something significant about it; something mundane and ordinary among the chaos and the sparks. A little slice of normality.

'Yeah, let's. What do you fancy?'

'Chinese?'

'Good choice.'

Ryan used his phone to log into one of the food delivery websites and find the nearest Chinese. He ordered a mix of everything while Alex poured them both a drink, then she sat down next to him on the sofa and turned so she was facing him.

'So, tell me about your busy day,' she said.

'A lot of travelling and a lot of network issues at various sites. Just a very long and boring day.' He paused for a second before adding, 'Better now though.' She saw his dimples appear in his cheeks as he smiled, beneath the stubble that had grown over the weekend.

She laughed. 'Very smooth.'

'Hey, it's true. I've been thinking about you a lot.' He rested his hand on her thigh and squeezed it gently.

'Is that right?'

He nodded. There was no hint of playfulness on his face as he looked at her. 'Yes. I thought about you all day today, and all day yesterday.'

She considered her position for a moment. His admissions felt as though he'd handed over some power. She wasn't naïve, she knew he was in control; he was the one who was unobtainable; he was the one calling the shots. She reasoned that if she didn't admit she felt the same – that she had thought of nothing *but* him since the moment he'd left – then she could hold on to his words and feel as though she had the smallest bit of control. It was as though she was adjusting the balance.

So, instead of responding, she simply took his hand and held it in hers for a moment before leaning in to him, her head resting on his chest. She breathed in the scent of him, the musky smell of his deodorant, and listened to the reassuring beat of his heart. She felt the tautness of his chest and the firmness in the arm he placed around her, and she let herself relax into him.

'Do you fancy watching a film?'

Alex sat up and looked at him, certain she must have misheard. 'Sorry?'

'Do you want to watch a film? A movie,' he clarified, clearly confused by her lack of comprehension.

'Yeah, I just didn't think…'

'Didn't think what?' There was a trace of a grin on his face as though he was playing with her, clearly amused by her confusion.

'I didn't think that would be something we'd do together.'

'Why not?'

Alex frowned at him, she felt sure he knew what she meant.

'Alex, I think a film is the least of my worries, don't you?'

'Well, when you put it like that.' She reached for the remote and clicked onto Netflix. 'What sort of thing do you like?'

'All sorts, really. What's your favourite film?'

'That's a tough one.' Alex thought for a moment. 'Anything Tom Hanks stars in... *The Green Mile*, *Bridge of Spies*, *Captain Phillips*...'

'Have you seen him in *News of the World*?'

'No, I don't think I have.'

'I've read some great reviews. I think it's on there...'

There was a knock at the door as she began scrolling through the selection of films. Ryan looked at her questioningly. 'That was fast.'

Alex frowned. She wasn't expecting their food for at least another half an hour, and it was rare for someone to knock at her door anyway – usually they would have to be buzzed in from the intercom, unless they'd arrived as someone else was leaving the building. Alex got up slowly, trying to mentally scroll through the list of people she knew who might turn up at her place without calling first, but she couldn't think of anyone.

When she got to the door, she placed her ear against it, listening. 'Hello?' she called, but there was no answer. She looked over her shoulder at Ryan who had stayed put, clearly a little unnerved at the thought of someone turning up and finding them together.

Alex opened the door slowly, but the hallway was empty. She stepped out into the corridor and looked both ways, checking, but there was no one there. Confused, she walked back inside and closed the door behind her. Ryan was looking at her from the sofa, his eyebrows raised.

'Someone must have got the wrong apartment,' she said, wondering if her words sounded as unconvincing as they felt. 'Happens a lot,' she lied.

'I suppose they're all pretty similar from the corridor.' Ryan turned back around and took over the remote, continuing to scroll through the films on the TV while Alex's heart raced. It could have been someone visiting a neighbour... or someone delivering a package... It would be easy to knock on the wrong door before quickly noticing your mistake.

'Found it,' Ryan called over. Alex realised she was still standing by the door.

'Oh, good.' She walked over to the sofa and sat down beside him, her head leaning against his shoulder. They settled into a comfortable silence, Alex trying to forget about whoever had knocked on her door.

Thirty minutes into the movie their food arrived, a notification on Ryan's phone reassuring them both who it was this time. Alex paused the TV while she got cutlery and plates from the kitchen and Ryan answered the door. It felt natural, as though they were moving seamlessly to the beat of domesticated bliss. They ate on the sofa with the movie playing, Alex's appetite returning.

When they'd finished, Ryan cleared the plates away and refilled their glasses before lying down on the sofa, his arm out waiting for Alex to slot in beside him. She looked at him – the top buttons of his shirt undone, his legs overhanging the two-seater sofa – and she couldn't believe that he didn't belong here, with her. Or perhaps he did. She joined him, her body fitting perfectly into the contours of his.

Behind her, in the space between the small of her back and her hip, she felt Ryan's phone vibrating. He didn't acknowledge it or try to answer, he just let it ring out. Five minutes later, it started again.

'Do you think you'd better get that?' Alex asked him, hoping he would tell her it was okay, that it was just a work call that could wait, but he didn't. He sat up and slid the phone out of his pocket, looking at the display. His eyes moved between the phone and Alex; he didn't need to tell her who it was. He stood and walked into the kitchen before answering. Alex paused the film and sat nursing her glass of wine, trying to discreetly listen in.

'Hello? Yeah, still stuck at work... I know, I know... Network issues… Did you try Calpol? Okay, okay, I'll be there as soon as I can.'

Alex didn't turn round, she sat looking at the frozen picture on the TV, waiting for him to tell her he had to leave.

'I'm sorry, I'm going to have to go.'

Alex looked up and smiled though she wasn't sure it was entirely convincing. 'I hope everything's okay?'

'It's Mia, she's not very well. High temperature.'

'Oh no, poor thing.' Alex stood and walked towards the door, disappointment raging inside her. She felt terrible – Mia was poorly and here she was, quietly resenting her.

'I'm sorry, Alex. I really wanted to stay.'

'It's fine, honestly. I hope she's feeling better soon.'

Ryan moved closer as though he was going to lean down and kiss her but then he seemed to change his mind, stopping quite suddenly. 'I think I'd better just…' He gestured towards the door. 'I'm not sure I would be able to tear myself away otherwise.'

'Go!' She tried to force a laugh, opening the door and stepping back to allow him through.

She watched him leave, his steps down the hallway more hurried than usual, then she closed the door and let her back rest against it. Tears pricked her eyes – sad, selfish tears she told herself she should not allow to fall. After all, she'd known this was how it would be, yet she'd failed to prepare herself for the reality of it.

Alex's back slid down the door until she was sat in a crumpled heap on the carpet, her vision distorted by the tears which kept coming. She pulled her knees to her chest and wrapped her arms around them. She felt silly for the enormity of the sadness she felt – it didn't fit the situation, it was too big; too heavy.

She closed her eyes tight. She couldn't bear to see all of the empty spaces around her.

CHAPTER THIRTEEN

Alex had spent the night on the sofa, puffy eyed and restless, and she'd woken in much the same way. She'd skipped the run so deeply ingrained in her routine, already allowing parts of herself to slip away. Exhausted, she'd stood under the shower until her skin prickled from the heat, the steam cascading around her. She'd gone through the motions of getting ready but without the usual care; her hair was flat, her silk blouse creased, her eyes sunken and red.

'What's up?' Chloe greeted her with a mug of coffee, bursting into the classroom and taking her by surprise. Alex had been sat at her desk with her head in her hands, her fingertips massaging her temples. She could feel a headache coming, a fogginess behind her eyes, the pressure building.

'I think I'm coming down with something.' She pulled a face, grimacing as she took the coffee.

'I hope it's not that sickness bug Nora had. Apparently it's going round.' Chloe was wearing a floral dress with a pair of Converse and had her bleached hair held back in a turquoise clip; she looked the polar opposite of Alex – bright and fresh and eager to start the day.

'I don't think so. Feels more like a cold.'

Chloe stuck her bottom lip out, a childlike sad face. 'Not long until we break up. Two weeks of freedom! Have you got anything planned?'

An image of Ryan popped into her mind and she quickly tried to quash it. 'Not a lot, no. I suspect I'll be here on some of the days.'

'Working?' Chloe perched on the edge of one of the little red tables.

'Just some of the displays and a bit of planning.'

'Alex, give yourself a break!'

She shrugged. 'What about you? Any plans?'

'We've booked to go to the coast for a couple of nights, I can't wait.'

Alex smiled and took a drink of her coffee. She hadn't eaten anything yet and her stomach rumbled with the emptiness, but she couldn't face anything; there was a lump in her throat that felt like an obstruction. Outside she could hear children playing and the low murmur of conversation. She checked her watch. 'We'd better let them in.'

She didn't expect to see Mia at school, not with how late Hannah had called Ryan the previous night saying she had a temperature, so when she opened the door to find Ryan stood at the front of the playground, his hand holding Mia's but his eyes set on her, Alex seemed to freeze mid-stride.

'I think I need a minute,' she said, stepping backwards and almost bumping into Chloe.

Chloe moved to one side and surveyed Alex, concern etched on her face. 'Why don't you go and have a sit down?'

'Yes, I think I ought to. Will you be okay for a few minutes?'

'Of course, take your time. You look a bit pale, actually.'

Alex retreated back into the classroom and then out into the narrow hallway. At the end, a small staffroom stood behind a wooden door. She considered going inside, getting a drink and having a sit down, but she could hear voices trailing out – the cleaner and the secretary, by the sound of it. She didn't want to get caught up in conversation, she needed a moment alone.

Instead, she darted into the toilet – the disabled one with its own sink and mirror – and locked the door behind her. She felt hot and clammy. She clutched the sink and looked at herself in the mirror – at the dark circles under her eyes and the smudges of mascara at the corners. She'd been neglecting herself, too wrapped up in something that could never be hers.

The previous night had been a stark reminder that this wasn't a fairy tale and there wouldn't be a happy ending. She grabbed a tissue and wet it, dabbing at the black blotches of make-up underneath bloodshot eyes. What was Ryan doing there; why was Mia in school? Wasn't she poorly? Alex wasn't sure why she'd had such a knee-jerk reaction to seeing him. All she knew was that she felt delicate in a way that unnerved her, as though one wrong move would reveal all to everyone.

There was a light knocking on the door, barely audible. 'Miss Vaughn?' came a voice. She couldn't place it at first. 'Alex?'

Alex cleared her throat and took a deep, steadying breath. 'Yes?'

'Are you all right?' It was Tess, the school secretary.

Alex opened the door. 'I'm okay,' she said, but even to her it didn't sound convincing. 'I think I'm coming down with something.'

Tess tilted her head to one side sympathetically. 'Oh dear, do you need to go home?'

'No, I'll be fine, I just needed a minute.'

'Mr Blake's asking to see you – Mia's dad. I tried to tell him you were unavailable but he says it's important.'

'Oh, right…'

Tess seemed to sense her unease. 'Don't worry, I'll tell him he'll have to speak–'

Alex interrupted. 'It's okay, I'll go and have a quick word with him before I go back to class. I think Mia's been having a few issues.'

'You're sure?'

'Yes, it's fine. Where is he?'

'He's waiting just outside.'

Alex nodded and inhaled deeply, trying to calm herself. 'Thank you.'

She walked past Tess and through reception, pressing the red button next to the door to release it. Ryan was leaning against a wall, his hands in his pockets. When he saw her he stood up straight and turned to face her. Before he could say anything she put a finger to her mouth and gestured for them to walk around the corner, where they couldn't be heard through the open window to reception.

'Are you okay?' he asked.

'Yes. How's Mia?'

He rolled his eyes. 'Absolutely fine.'

'Oh, well I'm glad she's recovered so quickly.'

'There was nothing wrong with her in the first place, it was just Hannah playing games.' He looked tired, perhaps more so than Alex did. He scratched the back of his neck and sighed.

'Does she...' Alex took a nervous glance over her shoulder before she continued. 'Does she suspect something?'

'I don't know. I don't think so.'

Alex panicked at how unsure he sounded. 'You don't *think* so?'

'I think she was just trying to get me home. I'd been working late for a long time before I met you and it isn't the first time she's done something like this.'

'Ryan, I can't do this here...'

'I'm sorry, I wanted to check you're okay? That *we're* okay?' When Alex didn't respond he glanced around to ensure no one was there before taking a step closer. 'It doesn't change anything. Not for me.'

'Okay.' She didn't know what to say. Had it changed anything?

Logistically, no. But emotionally, she had to admit it was more of a strain than she'd anticipated. She'd realised something important – she couldn't share him – but she didn't know what to do about it yet.

'Okay? So I can see you again?'

'If that's what you want.' She tried to keep her voice light and casual, as if the outcome of the conversation were of no great importance. The last thing she wanted was for Ryan to feel trapped by another woman.

'More than anything.'

Alex couldn't help but smile. He was saying all the right things.

'Look, I've been thinking...' He lowered his voice so Alex could only just hear what he was saying. 'What about spending a day together over the holidays?'

'But what about work and... everything else?'

'Han's taking Mia to her parents' house for a couple of days; I just need to check I can get it off work.'

'Okay.'

'I'll text you.'

Ryan smiled, his eyes lighting up in a way that made Alex forget everything that had happened between the previous night and that morning; every emotion she'd been through except for the simplicity of the relief she now felt. He raised his voice a little louder than was necessary: 'Thank you, Miss Vaughn. You've been very helpful.'

———

Alex didn't hear from Ryan until Friday, late afternoon, at least not directly: on Thursday morning, as she stepped out of her apartment and into the hallway, she'd found a beautiful bunch of flowers on the floor – lilies, wrapped in gold paper. She'd scooped them up and arranged them into a vase before she'd left.

At school the following day, she'd seen Ryan briefly as he dropped Mia off, but they hadn't had the opportunity to speak. She'd wanted to thank him for the flowers, but it would have to wait.

When the school day was over and the children had all left, she settled down at her desk and took her phone out of the drawer. There were a couple of messages – one from Emma asking her if she was free to meet up soon, and one from Ryan – just one sentence, but it was enough to make her beam.

How's Tuesday?

Alex hit reply.

Perfect.

She didn't want to push for times or plans yet, she was content enough just knowing that she would be seeing him. She replied to Emma telling her she would work out when she was free and get back to her. She felt bad; Emma was one of her oldest friends, the only one of their group who hadn't settled down and had kids besides her.

It had bonded them, in a way that she sometimes found a little forced and unnatural but had been convenient for them both. She still saw her wider group of friends on special occasions or for the odd night out, and they had a WhatsApp group where they would all chat from time to time, but Emma was the only one who had remained consistent through her adult life, until recently.

Her phone lit up again, Ryan's name popping up on her screen.

Will you be home this evening?

She wanted to wait to respond, to not seem as eager as she felt, but her fingers betrayed her, typing a response without letting her think.

Yes.

———

He turned up just after nine, dressed casually in a plain white T-shirt and jeans. There was a hunger in his eyes that she could feel, as though they'd both been waiting for this moment since he'd left her three days earlier.

'Thank you for the flowers,' she said between kisses.

He pulled back, his eyes narrowing. 'What flowers?'

Alex looked over her shoulder towards a vase of lilies displayed on her coffee table.

'They're lovely,' he said, 'but I didn't send them.'

They looked at each other for a moment, silently working out what that meant.

'Oh, right…' she said, her mind trying to work out who else could have sent them.

'You must have more than one admirer.'

Alex frowned. 'I don't think so.'

'Was there no note?'

Alex shook her head. 'They're probably from my mum.' She made a mental note to ask her the next time they spoke.

Ryan stayed until the early hours, Alex soon forgetting about the flowers, her mind filled instead with a torturous hope that one day they wouldn't have to hide away.

After he'd gone, she asked herself if it was worth it – the high followed by the low – but every time she tried to answer she got lost in thoughts of Ryan and she decided, maybe, that was the only answer she needed.

CHAPTER FOURTEEN

Alex's phone vibrated on the floor beside the bath. It was Monday evening and she'd been having a long soak, candles surrounding the tub and the scent of lavender bubbles filling the air. She dried her hands on a towel and picked up her phone. It was Ryan. She'd been expecting a message from him – he'd told her on Friday that he'd be in touch about Tuesday. They hadn't made any plans, but Alex was under the impression it would be a day spent at hers. After all, their options were limited.

> Pick you up at 9?

She frowned at the phone. Pick her up? She hit reply.

> Where are we going?

She watched as the little dots appeared on the screen indicating he was typing out a message. A moment later, there was a response.

> Put your walking boots on!

———

Alex was up with the sun though she wasn't sure she'd ever really slept. It wasn't her usual running day but she'd woken with an anxious energy that required movement. She decided to go for a short sprint around the block – a two-kilometre loop she used to track her times.

She put on a pair of shorts and a pink T-shirt, grabbed a quick drink of water, then slipped into her running shoes, tucking the key to the door into a little pocket on her waistband. She stretched briefly at the front of the apartment block then set off up the steady incline to the main road.

She started fast, the cool morning air awakening her skin and stinging her lungs. She turned left at the main road and left again when she came to Lees Avenue. There she would do a loop of a residential street before running back along the main road. She passed another runner and a dog walker but the streets were still quiet: her favourite time of day. The air felt cleaner, the world calmer. She breathed it in.

She let her mind wander to what it would be like to wake up with Ryan, to have him beside her in bed as the sun crept in. Then her thoughts switched to Hannah and the uncomfortable feeling that, somehow, she suspected Ryan was cheating on her. Alex couldn't put her finger on exactly what it was – there was no evidence to suggest she had any idea – but she couldn't shake the feeling.

She recalled Ryan's words from the day after he'd had to rush home: *'It was just Hannah playing games.'* Then her mind drifted to the flowers she'd received. They weren't from her mum – she'd asked her about them over the weekend – so Alex had concluded that they'd been left outside her door by mistake, intended instead for one of her neighbours. She'd thrown them away Sunday evening – the sight of them had made her feel uneasy.

She stopped her watch as she arrived back at her apartment

and told herself that she would put the niggling suspicions about Hannah to the back of her mind; she didn't want anything to taint the day ahead.

Alex took a long shower then blow-dried her hair and pulled on a pair of black leggings and a white Nike vest. She found her walking boots in the back of her wardrobe and grabbed her raincoat and backpack off a hook by the front door.

Just before nine she made her way downstairs to the front door – she didn't want Ryan to have to linger too long, when a lot of her neighbours would be filtering outside and into their own cars. She stood next to her little Peugeot, waiting, her backpack held in her hand.

A couple of minutes after nine she saw his black Honda SUV turn into her estate and pull into the bay next to her. She opened the passenger door and climbed inside.

'Morning.' Ryan was wearing a pair of black North Face shorts with a grey long sleeve top, the half-zip slightly undone.

'Morning.'

'I've brought coffee.' He gestured to two Costa takeaway cups in the holders near the gear stick.

'Thank you.' She took one and sipped at it.

'I didn't know what you liked,' he said, 'so I took a guess.'

It was a cappuccino with sugar, just how she liked it. 'Good guess.'

He reversed out of the spot; Alex watched the way that he did it with ease, one handed and smooth, not at all how she did it – stop starting and second guessing herself. He'd let his stubble grow and it bordered on a beard. It seemed to make him look younger, which wasn't what she usually found with men.

Her ex-partner, Lewis, had always looked considerably older with facial hair, and slightly dishevelled. But not Ryan. Alex was acutely aware that there wasn't a single thing she'd found to dislike about him; not even a tiny flaw which she could grasp on to and use to stop herself falling so hard and so fast. The only obstacle was his wife and child and she couldn't help thinking how unfair this was, to have found the perfect man who had accidentally ended up with a family of his own. Then she thought of Mia – sweet, lovely, innocent Mia – and Alex felt a pang of guilt for letting herself think this way.

'Where are we going?' she asked. He'd headed back out onto the main road and was driving away from the city centre.

'I thought we could head into the Peak District.'

'Are you sure it won't be too busy?'

Ryan seemed to think for a moment. 'I'm not going to lie, there's obviously a risk. This whole thing is a risk. But I want to take you places. I want to do things with you. I enjoy being with you, and I haven't had that feeling for a really long time. So for me, it's a small risk worth taking, because I get to be with you.' He indicated to turn left and Alex tried to suppress a smile. 'The question is: is it worth the risk for you?'

Alex knew she needed to consider her own feelings rather than get swept away with the emotion. Was it worth the risk? They both had things at stake – Ryan his family, Alex her career. Alex looked out of the window. There were so many shades of green, so many fields seeping into the next, divided by old stone walls which seemed to defy gravity. A solitary tree sat in the centre of a field to the left. A single crow sat perched on top of it, still against the movement of the leaves.

Alex didn't want to be alone anymore. She knew Ryan wasn't hers and that what they had could never be simple, but there was a part of her that held on to the hope that, if they carried on seeing each other for long enough, it would become impossible to walk away; that Ryan would fall for her in the same way she'd fallen for him.

'Yes,' she said finally. 'It's worth the risk.'

CHAPTER FIFTEEN

Ryan signalled right and drove up an incline to a small car park which wasn't visible from the road. It wasn't even half-full and this sparked a renewed confidence in Alex – perhaps this was okay; perhaps they wouldn't be seen.

An older couple with grey hair and matching beige gilets were stood at the parking machine trying to work out how to use it, walking poles held at their sides, and there was a lone woman with a black Labrador and a backpack just setting off on one of the trails. Ryan got out of the car and queued behind the couple using the machine.

After a couple of minutes Alex saw that he was talking to them, helping them punch in their registration number. She watched the way he conversed with them – his easy manner and charisma. The couple were smiling at him. He passed them their ticket and they waved goodbye.

A minute later, he was back at the car. 'Right, all sorted.' He slotted the ticket onto the dashboard and grabbed his backpack out of the boot. As she joined him at the back of the car, the boot still open, she noticed that, inside, were tell-tale signs of his family – a football decorated with Disney princesses, a woman's coat, a backpack with a picture of a unicorn on it. She turned away, pretending she hadn't seen, wishing she hadn't.

'Ready?' he asked.

'Ready!'

They walked down the hill to the road before crossing over to the other side. Ryan took her hand and held it in his and it felt to Alex as though it were the most natural thing in the world. They walked side by side as they crossed the water at Lady Bower Dam before taking the path which led up through a woodland, tall pine trees casting their shadow on the rocky trail.

'So, where are we exactly?' she asked, watching her footing as the terrain grew steadily steeper.

'Win Hill. I can remember climbing it as a kid with my granddad.'

'Really?'

'Yeah, one of my favourite memories of being a child.'

Alex felt touched that he'd brought her somewhere that meant so much to him. She wondered whether he'd ever brought Hannah there and, as though knowing what she was thinking, Ryan spoke again. 'I haven't been here since I was fifteen.'

They both pretended the insinuation behind this revelation was lost on them – just a casual statement between two people. In reality, Alex could think of nothing else. Why had he never brought Hannah there, to a place that meant so much to him? And did bringing Alex there so soon after meeting her mean what she hoped it did – that there was something between them, something more than an affair?

'Did your sister go with you?'

He laughed. 'No way, she's bone idle.'

'Just you and your granddad then?'

'Yeah, just the two of us.'

They stopped at a fallen tree and Ryan took off his backpack and extracted a bottle of water from it. He took a drink before passing it to Alex. She sipped at it while her eyes scanned the forest, imagining a younger Ryan there with his granddad.

'Is he still alive?'

'No, he died a few years ago. Had a heart attack while out on one of his walks.'

'Oh gosh, I'm so sorry.'

'He'd lived a good life, and what a way to go, doing something you love. He always used to tell me not to make any excuses when it came to happiness. But it's not really that simple, is it?'

'No, nothing ever is.' She passed the bottle of water back to Ryan. They were standing next to each other but with their eyes fixed on the trees rather than each other. 'Look, Ryan, there's no pressure from me, you know that, right?'

He turned towards her and held her hands. 'I know. And you've no idea how grateful I am for that.'

She wanted to ask him whether he was having a change of heart; whether he thought there was a way in which he could leave Hannah, if not now, then in the future. She was prepared to wait for him. She knew it was less about him having the strength to make the decision and more about him being able to live with it. She decided to let it go.

They carried on, following the path through the dense woodland until it fell away, shifting into moorland, wild and untamed. They could see the peak from there and Alex took a moment to observe it, her hands on her hips as she caught her breath. She turned to look for Ryan but his gaze was elsewhere, away from the peak, scanning the tops of the trees which sat below them. Beyond the forest, the view was drenched in a golden glow cast by the high sun, the water from the dam sparkling as it caught the light. Ryan put his hand on the small of her back and bent down to her ear. His breath was warm against her neck.

'Beautiful, isn't it?'

'It really is.'

She rested her head against his shoulder. 'Thank you for bringing me here.'

'Thank you for coming. I've been wanting to come back here for a while but…' His voice trailed off, the sentence hanging there for her to catch.

She stood up straight and turned to face him, waiting for him to meet her eyes. 'But?'

'But I've been putting it off, I suppose. It brings back a lot of memories.'

'Happy memories, by the sound of it?'

'Yes. Happy memories.'

They carried on towards the peak, through the rough grass of the moorland and over the rocky terrain. As they stood at the top, by the pillar which told them they'd made it, she placed her hand on her chest and felt the steady beat of her heart, Ryan's hand clasped tightly in hers.

———

The sky was an inky blue when they pulled up outside Alex's. She was exhausted but felt more relaxed and content than she had done in a long time. She rested her head to one side and looked at him, wanting to invite him inside without speaking the words. His hands were resting on the steering wheel as though deep in thought, his eyes fixed on the windscreen, though Alex suspected he was actually looking at something that wasn't there, something deep inside his memories – Mia perhaps. Or Hannah.

'You know,' Ryan turned to her, the spell he was under broken. 'I haven't got to go home tonight.'

It was all Alex had wanted to hear, yet now that she was hearing it she realised that it came tinted with an insinuation – that every other night he *would* have to go home. She swallowed, trying to sink the thought. Before she had chance to reply, Ryan's phone vibrated in his pocket. He took it out and as he looked at the display he sighed, his eyes telling Alex all she needed to know – he needed to answer.

'It won't take long.'

She wasn't sure if she was supposed to get out and wait, to linger around outside her apartment waiting for him to finish talking to his wife. Ryan made no move to get out, to seek the privacy he could easily get on the other side of the door, so she stayed where she was, her hands wringing in her lap.

'Hi...' She could hear a woman's voice on the other end of the line – Hannah's – and she could make out certain words, but not the whole conversation. 'Yeah, busy... How's Mia?' He laughed at something Hannah said. 'She knows her own mind, that's all, Han... Yeah just going to grab something to eat then get an early night...' His eyes crossed to Alex at this, she could feel them on her but she didn't reciprocate. It felt too private, as though she would be intruding. 'All right, yeah I'll ring you tomorrow. Night.'

No '*I love you*', she noticed, and it was this observation that carried her as she got out of the car. When she looked up, she stopped mid-stride then took a step back, her eyes fixed on the side of her car.

'Shit!'

Ryan walked round to stand beside her, following her gaze to the big ugly scratch that ran down the side of her car. He took a step towards it and bent down, brushing his fingertips over the top of it. Then he looked up at the side of the building. 'No cameras?'

Alex shook her head. It was a clean scrape, no paintwork from another car, and it ran the whole length of the driver's side. To her novice eye, it looked deliberate. 'Do you think someone did this on purpose?' she asked, not sure if she wanted to hear the answer.

Ryan took a deep breath before answering, his eyes flitting between Alex and the car. 'Maybe.'

'Do you think…' she began, hoping that he'd know what she was suggesting without having to say it.

'It can't have been Hannah. She's in Kent. Besides, there's no way that she could know.'

Alex wasn't sure whether there was a hint of defensiveness in his voice or whether he was simply stating a fact, but it made her immediately regret bringing it up.

'Could be kids,' he offered. 'Or it could be genuine and someone just didn't bother to stop.'

'Yeah, I suppose.'

'You could check if any of the houses over there have one of those camera door bells?' he suggested, pointing over to a row of town houses facing them.

'I'll ask around tomorrow.'

Ryan crouched down, feeling the scratch again. 'It might polish out, could be worth a try?'

Alex smiled, wanting to forget about it for now and enjoy having Ryan with her for the night. He stood, his eyes skimming their surroundings to check they were alone, then he reached out and took her hand in his.

'Or…' he said, 'we could forget about this for now, and enjoy tonight.'

'You read my mind.'

CHAPTER SIXTEEN

A lex slept heavily, the contented sleep of happiness, the scratch on her car buried under the weight of her feelings for Ryan. When she woke it was to darkness, the sun yet to rise. Ryan's silhouette was visible in the creamy light of the moon and, as her eyes adjusted and she moved closer, she could just make out his features. His strong straight nose. His dark eyebrows and high cheekbones. The smooth contours of his muscle. To her, he was perfect, in every way but his availability.

The light crept in through the window as the sun rose, hazy beams looking for spaces to fill. She tried to savour every aspect of him being there with her; it had been such a long time since someone had spent the night in her bed. She'd fallen asleep on his shoulder, his arm wrapped around her, the palm of her hand flat against his chest. She'd enjoyed feeling the rise and fall of it, the rhythm of his heartbeat and the way his breathing altered as he drifted off to sleep – light at first then gradually deeper and slower. At some point during the night they'd changed positions. Separated. She'd reached out and felt for him, moving closer, needing to feel him next to her.

His eyes flickered as the room lightened; he stretched an arm out and shuffled his feet under the covers.

'Morning.' He turned to face her.

'Morning.'

He reached over to the nightstand beside the bed where he'd left his watch, looking at it before turning back to her.

'What time is it?' she asked.

'Still early.'

'Haven't you got to get to work?'

'Nothing in the diary until eleven.' He kissed her gently and she was suddenly conscious of the way she must look; her hair wild and eyes groggy, and she hadn't yet cleaned her teeth.

'I need a shower,' she said, trying to hide her face against his chest.

His hand brushed at her thigh. 'Fancy some company?'

He followed her into the bathroom, the pair of them giggling, and all she could think about was how she could get used to this.

How she *wanted* to get used to this.

They ate breakfast together on the sofa – bagels and coffee – and watched a morning news show on TV that neither of them really listened to. She kept looking at the time, wondering when he would have to leave. She didn't want to ask him; it was as though they were both pretending the outside world and its obstacles didn't exist, and she didn't want to burst the pretence and have reality come crashing down around them.

'Have you ever lived with anyone?' His question came out of the blue. There had been no build-up to it, no conversation about a similar topic or mention of previous relationships.

'Yes, once.'

He nodded but didn't press for more information. She wondered if she should offer it – she knew his wife and taught his daughter, it seemed only fair to share a little bit of her own life. 'A few years ago now. We had a house in Nottingham but we were only renting...' She wasn't sure why she told him this particular piece of information but she didn't know what else she should tell him.

Lewis was the kind of man you could chat to at a party but would promptly forget afterwards. You could take him home to your parents and know they would get along just fine, but out with your friends you would worry that he seemed boring. But what Alex hadn't realised until far too late into their relationship was that Lewis was also the kind of man used to getting his own way. While things were ticking along, going the way he liked, Lewis was easy going. Amenable. It blinded her, the two sides to him.

When Alex had told him that she didn't want to relocate for his job, he couldn't understand how a world existed where he had to choose between two things, and lose one of them in the process. She'd stood listening as his placidity had slipped away; as the mask had been removed, revealing a darker side to Lewis that Alex hoped never to see again.

They'd met at a mutual friend's wedding seven years earlier; they'd both had too much to drink and swapped numbers out of obligation more than anything – they were the only single people there and Chelsea, the bride, had insisted they'd hit it off. And they did, kind of. At least at first. But it was as though Alex had slowly been opening her eyes to who he really was, at his core. So she'd told him that he should go, that he should move wherever his work took him, but that she would not be following him.

'What happened?' Ryan asked. He was playing with her hair, his arm around her shoulders as they lay next to each other on the sofa, Ryan's feet overhanging the end.

'Erm, I guess it just ran its course. He wanted to move and I didn't want to go with him.'

Now that she thought about it, had she ever really loved Lewis? Maybe it was just companionship, but she hadn't had much to compare it with. Until Ryan.

'Do you…' His voice seemed to betray his usual confidence

and Alex thought he sounded shy, or maybe a little embarrassed. He paused but his fingers continued to twist and twirl her hair. 'Do you want to meet someone? Do you want to settle down and have kids? I know it's probably not something I should be asking but...' He spoke quickly, as though needing to get the words out while they were available to him, afraid that otherwise he would lose them.

Alex didn't know what to say. She wasn't sure what his angle was. Was he asking her because he was curious if that's what she was searching for with other people, or because he wondered if that's what she wanted from him? She couldn't work it out.

'I try not to think about it. My plans never really seem to work out in that regard.'

His hand settled against her arm, his fingers tired of running through her hair. 'I want you to be happy.'

She sat up and looked right at him. 'I *am* happy.'

She chose not to add: *'when I'm with you.'*

CHAPTER SEVENTEEN

The holidays dragged, the days seeming impossibly long. Ryan had left just after ten on Wednesday morning and, a week later, she still hadn't heard anything from him. Nor had she done anything about her car and the big ugly scratch down the side of it. She wasn't sure whether it was because she lacked the mental capacity required to deal with it, or whether it was something deeper: was she scared that, somehow, it was linked to their affair?

More than once over the past week, she'd had the odd sensation that someone was watching her. She tried to tell herself she was being paranoid, overthinking the possible consequences of the affair and the reason behind Ryan's sudden silence, but she couldn't shake it. A couple of times, she felt sure she'd heard a shuffling outside her front door, in the corridor that was usually so quiet. She'd edged over to listen, placing her ear against the smooth wood surface.

Once, she thought she could hear breathing coming from outside, slow and deep, and she'd taken herself away and paced her apartment, telling herself how ridiculous she was being.

When she'd gone back with renewed determination and flung open the door, it was to an empty corridor. But the absence of something more sinister did little to appease the disquiet that hung over her.

Waiting to hear from Ryan was torturous. It felt deliberately cruel. Countless times she'd written out a text on her phone, but whenever she'd thought about pressing send, she imagined every possible catastrophic situation that could come from it. It usually entailed Hannah finding the messages and reporting her to the school, and Ryan refusing to ever speak to Alex again. There was a constant ache in her chest – sometimes dull and tight and other times sharp like glass – but she refused to acknowledge it was her heart, because that would imply that Ryan had broken it.

Alex was lying on the sofa watching *Friends* repeats on Netflix when her phone pinged. It was already in her hands; she'd taken to walking round the apartment with it, keeping it beside her in bed and on top of the sink while she showered. She unlocked it with her thumbprint and saw Emma's name pop up on the screen.

> Hi babe. Fancy dinner and drinks tonight? Owen and I have split up, could do with a night out.

Alex rolled her eyes. She could have told her this would happen weeks ago, but then perhaps Alex wasn't in a position to judge. She began typing a message, forming an excuse about having plans with her mum, when she stopped herself. Maybe this was exactly what she needed. Emma had divulged her relationship problems to her enough times over the years, maybe it was her turn to offload.

And she could do with getting out of the apartment. Apart from her runs – which had been lacklustre compared to usual – she hadn't been out. She'd ordered a food delivery and a couple of takeaways but her appetite had dwindled, the knot in her stomach taking up the space usually reserved for food. She hadn't even seen her mum. She'd called her twice and Carol had seemed happy that she was deviating from her usual routine, suspecting – Alex thought – that she was seeing the mystery man they'd spoken about.

Alex typed back a response.

> Sorry to hear about Owen. Sounds good, meet at our usual at 7?

Emma replied straight away.

> See you there!

———

Alex caught the bus into Nottingham then walked to the bar they usually met at. Emma wasn't there yet, she'd texted to say she was running a little late, so Alex found a table in the corner of the room and sat herself down. The bar was called The Garden Room and was set out almost like a greenhouse – lots of glass and greenery, flowers adorning the tables and hanging from the walls. Before nine was happy hour – cocktails were buy one get one free. They'd got into the habit of arriving early enough to take advantage, back when nights out were a regular thing.

Alex put her phone on the table and checked there were no messages or missed calls. Nothing. She'd searched for both Ryan and Hannah on Facebook and Instagram over the past week, but Ryan had neither and Hannah's was so private that she could see nothing but her name and profile photo, which was Mia. Alex was desperate for information. She felt pathetic. She was considering having another look when she became aware of someone standing in front of her.

'Hi.' Alex looked up to find a man smiling down at her. 'Alex, isn't it?'

Alex regarded the man before her: there was something vaguely familiar about him, but she was struggling to place him.

'You attended my well-being course a couple of months ago,' he said, trying to jog her memory. He was holding a bottle of beer and he passed it awkwardly from one hand to the other, waiting for her to respond.

'Oh,' she said, her brain scrambling to recall it. 'Yes, the one at the old church?'

'That's the one. I was the course leader – I'm Henry,' he said, his hand tapping his chest.

She'd been asked to attend the training back in January by the head teacher, Mrs Harlow. Alex could recall the journey more than anything because it had started to snow and she'd struggled to see on the winding roads, the deluge of white almost blocking her view through the windscreen.

The course had been one of those to add to her CV rather than anything else. If she could remember rightly, the aim had been all about retaining staff, with much of the information being provided via a mind-numbing PowerPoint which told them all what they already knew but apparently needed to hear collectively in a freezing cold room. She'd rolled her eyes at the mundanity of it all and had spent much of the day with her mind elsewhere, watching the clock which ticked loudly from the walls of the old church.

'Oh yes, it was a good course,' she lied.

'Thank you.' He smiled, looking a little sheepish. 'To be completely honest, I tried to catch you at the end but you left in such a hurry.'

She'd had a date. She could remember the course running over and she'd needed to get home and shower before meeting a guy whose name she now could not recall. She'd been watching the snow stop-start all day through the old church window, a blanket of white covering the gardens outside.

'That's right, it was snowing.' Alex glanced over his shoulder, wondering where Emma had got to.

Henry smiled, cheeks flushing slightly. 'Yes, I'd wanted to ask you if you fancied going out for a drink.'

'Oh.' She felt flustered. This man had appeared from nowhere and within a matter of minutes he'd asked her out. It was uncomplicated and simple yet not at all what she was used to.

'Sorry, do you have a boyfriend?'

'Well... no.' She tucked her hair nervously behind her ear.

Henry stood awkwardly while he waited for her to elaborate. He was older than her by perhaps a few years but he had a boyish charm about him; a wave to his dark brown hair and a cheekiness to his smile. He was wearing a blue checked shirt with jeans and a pair of wire-framed glasses which he kept pushing up his nose with his forefinger. Ordinarily, she would have given him her number and been open to seeing where it might lead, but something was holding her back. Or someone. She glanced nervously at her phone.

Henry continued. 'Look, why don't I give you my number? If you decide you fancy that drink – great. If you don't, then you can just delete it.'

Alex laughed. 'Okay, that might work.' She unlocked her phone and handed it over. When he passed it back she saw that he'd saved his number under 'Henry – may or may not call.'

'Have a good night,' he said, then he disappeared off into the growing crowds.

Emma arrived ten minutes later, flustered and red eyed. She'd been crying, Alex could tell, and it almost made her regret coming. She wasn't in the mood to hear about someone else's problems, she wanted to offload hers, to tell someone who wasn't related to the school or the community about what was going on – adjusting a few details, of course.

'I need a drink.' Emma sighed. 'Actually, I need two.'

Alex ordered a round of espresso martinis and pina coladas

which came in enormous glasses she struggled to balance on the tray. When she sat back down again, Emma took a deep breath then said: 'Please tell me you have some gossip because I do *not* want to talk about Owen tonight. I am *done*.' She slammed her hands against the table to accentuate the point and Alex relaxed slightly – maybe she wouldn't be a sobbing mess after all.

'Actually, yes. But it has to stay between me and you, okay?'

'Consider me intrigued.'

'I mean it, Em. No one else knows what I'm about to tell you.'

'Babe, you can trust me.'

Alex had never had to test Emma's trustworthiness before. They'd gossiped and shared stories about bad dates but she'd never confided anything like this in her. She felt the overwhelming need to tell someone about Ryan; it was as though she'd reached her limit and she couldn't possibly make sense of it all in her own head anymore. She needed to transfer some of the burden.

'Okay.' She took a long drink of the espresso martini and felt the effects almost instantly, the bitterness gathering in her throat. 'I've kind of been seeing someone.'

Emma clapped her hands together excitably. 'I *knew* it! I knew there was something going on! You've been really quiet.'

'It's not as simple as it sounds.'

Emma raised her eyebrows and leaned forwards across the table. The bar was getting busier and the noise from the conversation getting louder. 'Oh?'

'He's married.' She put her hands to her face as she said it then parted her fingers so that she could just make out Emma's reaction. Her mouth opened, her eyes widened, but there was a grin on her face that spoke to her curiosity.

'Alex!'

'I know, I know. It just… happened. We didn't go looking for it and he's never done anything like this before.'

'So he says.'

'And I believe him.'

'Does he have kids?'

'Yes. One. I know, it's terrible. *I'm* terrible. But I really like him, Em. In fact, I think it's more than that. I think I'm falling in love with him.'

'Is he going to leave his wife?'

'It's complicated. He wants to, but he's scared she'll stop him seeing his kid.'

'Bullshit!'

'No, it's true.'

'And how do *you* know?'

'I know her, kind of. I've met her.'

'Oh my God, Alex, does his kid go to your school?'

'What! No, don't be ridiculous.'

'Then how do you know his wife as well?'

'Just through mutual friends.'

Emma looked at her sceptically. 'You're playing with fire, babe. If this *is* a guy you know through schoo–'

Alex interrupted. 'It isn't!'

'Okay, okay, but if he *is* linked to the school – to your job – you need to end it. Seriously, no man's worth you losing the career you've worked so hard for.'

Alex sighed and her eyes impulsively looked back to her phone.

'I'm not saying it to be mean. I'm saying it as a friend.'

'I know. It's probably not even in my control anymore. I haven't heard from him since last week.'

'So let me guess, you've just sat around waiting for him to call, wasting your time off?'

'Pretty much.'

'Alex, you're better than that.'

'I can't help it, Em! I've honestly never felt like this before, it's driving me mad.'

'Then you need to find a way of getting over him, or at least a way of taking your mind off him.'

In the distance, Alex could just make out the back of Henry's head, the slight wave to his hair as he stood talking to a small group of men. She took her phone off the table and dropped it into her bag, then picked up the half-finished cocktail and drained the rest.

CHAPTER EIGHTEEN

Alex woke with a dryness in her mouth which made her gag. The room felt hot and the air stale. She tried to swallow but her throat felt obstructed and she began to cough. She sat up and her feet found the floor, her clothes in a pile next to the bed. Her head was fuzzy, her memories of the night before blurry and fragmented. It made her panic. Had she texted Ryan? She scrambled around on the floor for her phone but couldn't find it. Her whole body seemed to ache; she felt battered and bruised. She sat back down on her bed and winced.

'Morning.'

Alex screamed. Henry had appeared at the bedroom door with two mugs in his hands. When he realised she was naked he quickly turned away, spilling dark liquid from the mugs. 'Shit, sorry.'

She grabbed frantically at the sheets from her bed, pulling and wrapping them around herself. Henry was fully clothed, his hair sticking up and his eyes hazy with sleep.

'You scared me!'

He turned back to face her. 'Yes, I can see that. I'm sorry.'

Alex held the sheet around herself while desperately trying to search for memories of how he'd ended up in her apartment. She could remember them dancing together but couldn't recall where. She could remember seeing him in a bar with flashing lights and laughing at something he'd said. But try as she might, she could not remember how they'd ended up in her apartment together.

'What are you doing here?'

'I heard movement. Thought you'd need a drink.' He held one of the mugs out for her and she took it, cradling it in her hands.

'But what are you doing *here*... in my apartment?'

'Oh, you don't remember?'

Alex shook her head.

'Well... you were a little unsteady on your feet. I was worried about you getting home so we took a cab together. I was going to leave but you kept asking me to stay, so I slept on the sofa. I hope that's okay.'

Alex was relieved to hear they hadn't shared a bed, but she was mortified that she couldn't remember.

'I'm sorry; I must have drunk too much.'

The black hole in her memories scared her. She put her coffee on the bedside table then squeezed the bridge of her nose. She could feel a headache coming. Henry shifted his weight, looking a little awkward as he lingered by the door. He seemed to be avoiding looking directly at her and Alex suddenly realised that the sheet had come loose, exposing her hip and leg as she sat perched on the edge of the bed.

'Shit,' she said, quickly adjusting it.

Henry grabbed her robe off the back of the door and handed it to her, his gaze still averted. 'Here...'

She took it from him and slipped it on. 'Jesus, my head's throbbing.'

'Can I get you anything? Painkillers? Some food?'

'No, definitely not food.' She held her hand to her stomach and felt it churning. She shouldn't have drunk on an empty stomach, it was a stupid mistake and she should know better. 'I need water,' she said. The smell of the coffee was making her gag. 'And a shower.'

'Let me get you some water.'

He left the room in a hurry. Alex couldn't help feeling sorry for him, he looked flustered and embarrassed when all he'd done was try to make sure she got home safely. While he was busy in the kitchen Alex took a quick shower, washing the blurred make-up from her face and the smell of alcohol from her skin. She lathered the soap and rubbed it in, and as she did so she noticed several bruises. They were dotted around her thighs and her arms, dark red turning purple, small but angry looking. What the hell had she been doing? She felt more than hungover. She felt as though she'd been in a fight. And lost.

She cleaned her teeth and brushed her damp hair, trying to make herself feel slightly more human, but it didn't work. Her head was pounding and her whole body throbbed. She took a couple of paracetamols out of the bathroom cabinet and swallowed them down with some water straight from the tap, then she put on a pair of jogging bottoms and a T-shirt and walked tentatively into the kitchen, her head dizzy and her stomach gurgling. The room seemed to be moving as she put one foot in front of the other and she found herself needing to place her hand against the solid foundations of the wall.

'Here we go.' Henry was stood waiting for her beside the kitchen table. He passed her a mug with 'Best Teacher Ever' written brightly on the side. 'Couldn't find the glasses,' he said, smiling.

'Thank you.' She sipped at it, her stomach protesting, then she sat down on one of the wooden chairs. 'I feel terrible. I'm covered in bruises. What the hell happened last night?'

'You were... struggling to walk. Falling over a lot. Falling into things.'

Alex winced at his words. She felt like she was eighteen again, partying at university without fear of repercussions. 'Jesus.'

'I had to pick you up a few times. Off the floor.' He looked down as he said the last part, as though reliving the memory caused him significant embarrassment. Shame, even.

Alex shook her head then quickly realised that was a mistake; it caused a wave of nausea.

Henry inhaled, held his breath for a second as though deliberating. 'I'd better get going.'

'But how are you going to get home?'

'I'll walk, it's not far.'

'I can drive you, it's the least I can do.'

'No, honestly, it's fine. I could use the fresh air.'

'I'm sorry about last night. I realise I didn't exactly make a great impression. I've had a difficult few weeks and I drank too much...'

'Alex, you don't have to explain, you're allowed to go out and let your hair down. I just got the impression that you're not entirely single at the moment and I don't want to get in the middle of anything.'

'No, that's not true. Why, what did I say last night?'

'You don't remember?'

'No, I'm sorry, like I said I must have drunk way too much.'

Henry grabbed the back of the chair opposite Alex and looked down at the table as he spoke, seemingly unable to look Alex in the eye. 'You kept saying "fuck Ryan" and when I asked who Ryan was you said that you loved him.'

Alex closed her eyes, trying to shut out what she was hearing. What a disaster of a night. She wondered briefly where Emma was and why she hadn't been the one escorting her home safely, but then Alex was pulled back to the present.

'I... I shouldn't have said that. I'm sorry. It's not true, he's just a guy I was seeing and I'm not anymore.' Even as she spoke the words she wasn't sure if she believed them. Was it over? She knew that if Ryan turned up right now she would struggle to tell him the same thing. But Ryan wasn't here – Henry was. She couldn't put her life on hold for a man who couldn't offer her a future.

Henry raised his eyebrows. 'Really? Because I'm too old to get caught up in anything messy.'

'Really.' She sounded convincing and she wondered whether some part of her truly meant it, a part that knew what a catastrophic fuck-up the whole Ryan thing had been in the first place.

'Okay. Well, why don't you text me when you're feeling better, and maybe we could arrange that drink?'

'You still want to go out with me?'

He laughed lightheartedly. 'I don't think one drunken night defines who we are. Of course I want to take you out. But a proper date this time.'

'Okay. It's a date.'

CHAPTER NINETEEN

Alex surprised herself by not immediately checking her phone once Henry had left. She got back into bed and tried to sleep but memories of the previous night kept coming back to her, a constant trickle of embarrassment. She could remember texting Henry from a bar she'd moved on to with Emma, telling him to come and find her. She could remember Emma dancing with one of his friends, a tall gangly looking man with a shaved head and a tattoo of someone's name on his inner forearm. She could remember falling over in the street and laughing uncontrollably as someone tried to help her up – Henry, maybe. How could she have got into such a state?

After tossing and turning for what seemed like hours, Alex decided to get up. In the lounge, she found a half-empty bottle of vodka sat on top of the coffee table, two empty glasses next to it, and, scattered around them, the contents of her bag. The sight of the clear liquid made her stomach churn – she couldn't remember opening it the previous night, or drinking it. She picked up her phone, unlocking it with the intention of texting Emma about the night before. Instead, sat waiting for her were five messages – two from Emma and three from Ryan. Alex's stomach tensed. She stared at the screen for a while, at the letter R with the number three next to it. She didn't dare click on it – what if it was a message to tell her it was over? Or that Hannah had found out? The uncertainty was better than the finality of knowing it was over, surely?

She paced about with the phone in the palm of her hand, backwards and forwards between the lounge and the bedroom. She needed to move, despite the pounding in her head and the aching in her limbs; it was something primal, the fight or flight response taking over as the adrenaline surged through her veins. Then, as though her thumb had made the decision for her, she clicked on to the messages.

The most recent were the two from Emma which had been sent just over an hour ago.

> Fucking hell, babe, what the hell happened last night?

> You feeling okay?

Alex couldn't take the words in, she could only focus on finding out what the other messages said – the ones from Ryan. She clicked on to them to see the first was sent at just before 10pm.

> Are you home? I'm sorry I've been absent, I'll explain when I see you.

Then, almost an hour later:

> I'm outside, can you let me in?

The last message wasn't received until just after midnight.

> I'm glad you got home safely.

'Shit! Shit! Shit!' She was shouting at her phone, her eyes on the messages. She didn't know what to do. Had Ryan waited for her the previous night, hidden from view in the parking bay next to hers? Did he see her enter the apartment block with Henry?

She felt as though she'd been caught cheating, despite knowing that's not what this was. How could she cheat on a married man? They'd expressed no loyalties to each other; they both knew what this was – an affair. He had a wife he went home to every night. So why did it feel as though she'd done something wrong? Why did she feel an overwhelming need to apologise to him?

Her mind was in overdrive. It was Thursday – he'd be at work, so it was safe to text him, wasn't it? She hit reply but her mind went blank, what could she possibly say? She'd never been good at communicating over text, she found the whole thing so devoid of feeling. Things could easily be misinterpreted, the tone altered between sending and receiving. She needed to see him, to talk face to face.

Can we meet?

She pressed send before allowing herself to analyse it or think about the consequences. Then she waited; she waited for those little dots, her breathing shallow and her cheeks flushed. A couple of minutes later she saw them. He was typing.

I'll come round after work tonight.

She felt the relief wash away some of the tension, her jaw unclenching, her shoulders dropping. It wasn't complete, but it was a start.

———

He arrived earlier than she'd anticipated. It was just after six when her phone buzzed, a message from Ryan telling her he was outside. She pressed the little button on the intercom to let him in downstairs, then she listened for the sound of his footsteps coming down the hall, opening the door to see him striding confidently towards her. She had to fight the urge to run to him. His eyes looked tired and groggy and as he drew closer she could see dark circles underneath them which weren't usually there.

'Hey.' She stood back to let him in and as he passed she noticed him smiling thinly at her; not the smile she was used to, but the slightly wounded and weary smile someone gives to offer reassurance, even when it's clear that all is not well. When she shut the door he stepped towards her, his hand resting briefly on her arm. She wasn't sure what she'd been expecting, but it wasn't this.

'Do you want a drink?' she asked. They were both lingering by the door a little awkwardly and she wondered whether this was his way of holding back, of not committing himself to staying.

'No, thank you. I haven't got long.'

'Oh, okay. Shall we sit down?'

She felt reassured when he nodded, walking over to the sofa and sitting down – he was staying. They sat side by side, Alex turning herself round so she was facing him, her knee up on the cushion. She still felt hungover, her head sore and her stomach unsettled, but it was nothing compared to the emotional turmoil.

'I'm sorry about last night, I...'

'What are you sorry for?' He was sitting forward, his knees apart and his forearms resting on his thighs. He reminded Alex of someone in a hospital waiting room – someone who was expecting bad news.

'I didn't know you were going to be here... I didn't see you...'

She realised to her embarrassment that she was crying. All the emotion of the day had mixed with the many emotions of the week and now they were spilling over. She was powerless to stop them.

'Alex, you have *nothing* to be sorry for.' He grabbed her hand and held it but remained on the edge of his seat. '*I'm* the one who should be apologising. I should have been in touch… or maybe I should never have started this.' He rubbed a hand over his face and exhaled slowly. 'I never wanted to hurt you. You deserve to be happy and if that guy last night is able to offer you that then, well, I think you should go for it.'

'You want me to start seeing someone else?'

'Yes. No. I don't know.' Ryan repositioned himself on the sofa, turning round to look her in the eyes. 'The thought of you with someone else kills me, Alex. But I'm married. I go home to my wife every night and I know that can't be easy for you.'

'No, it's not.'

'I don't want you to be upset because of me. I don't want you to put your life on hold.'

Alex wanted to tell him that she *wanted* to put her life on hold for him, that she would do anything for him because she loved him, but she couldn't bring herself to say the words because, deep down, she wasn't sure if they'd be reciprocated.

'I've had a great time with you. But I know where this is leading and I'm not sure if it's good for either of us.'

'How do you know where this is leading? What does that even mean?' She felt angry, angry at Ryan for trying to make decisions for her and angry at the world for her being in this situation in the first place, competing for a love that could never be hers.

'Because I can feel it.' He put a hand on his chest. 'This isn't just a fling. It never was.'

Alex wiped away the tears but new ones stung her eyes. She was trying to cling on to her dignity, to hold in the words that were trying to escape – the ones that told him she didn't care if she got hurt at some distant point in the future, that she would deal with that then, not now; that all she wanted was to be with him, in whatever way she could.

'Is that what you came here to tell me last night?'

'No. Last night I'd come to see you. I parked up and waited – I thought maybe you hadn't checked your phone – then I was about to leave when I saw a taxi pulling up outside. Seeing you with that guy, it confirmed to me what I already knew – I'm in too deep. I can't think straight, Alex. All I can think about is you and when I'll next see you or speak to you.'

'I feel the same way.' Her voice was barely above a whisper, salty tears falling to her lips as she spoke.

He leaned forward and put his hand on her cheek, wiping the tears away with his thumb. 'I'm sorry I haven't been in touch. I was going to text you last weekend – I wanted to see you – but Hannah booked a last-minute break camping in the Lake District and I had no signal. Then Mia went horse riding and fell off and broke her arm.'

'Oh God, is she okay?'

'She's fine now. Her arm's in a cast. But I wanted you to know it wasn't an intentional silence. I thought about you every minute of every day.'

Alex moved closer to him, tentatively at first and then, when he held her gaze, with more confidence. She knelt beside him then moved onto his lap, her lips finding his. A part of her was waiting for him to tell her he had to go, that this wasn't a good idea, but the words never came. Instead, his hands searched her body, looking for answers she wasn't sure he would find. It was as though they both needed this, but she couldn't decide whether it was borne from hunger or a need for clarity or, perhaps, a prerequisite of his goodbye.

Her aching heart was telling her it was the latter, and she savoured every moment because of it.

CHAPTER TWENTY

Alex had to stop during her morning run; her chest felt tight and her lungs burned from the exertion. She leaned against a wall to catch her breath, the brick rough and cool beneath her hands. She pushed into it, pleased to have something physical to feel. She looked up at the dusky sky and tried to suppress an overwhelming urge to scream into it, to try to displace some of what she was feeling.

She didn't want to have to endure this anymore, she was drained, her mind unable to focus and her body losing its anchor. Routine and predictability had always been vital to her, but it had all slipped away. She was sleeping in the day and awake during the night. She couldn't eat and, when she did, it was usually something unhealthy and swallowed down with alcohol.

She felt she was losing so much of herself that she was surprised when she looked in the mirror and saw the same reflection – sunken cheeks and red eyes but still unarguably her. She could not work out how to get the pieces of herself back, it was as though they were scattered in places that were out of reach.

On her way home, her pace barely more than a walk, she

suddenly felt unnerved, as though the air itself had changed, becoming charged with something which startled her. She stopped mid-stride, overcome with the feeling that someone was lingering nearby. Watching. It tingled her skin and caught her breath. She could feel eyes burrowing into her as sure as if she was staring right at them.

She looked behind her, suddenly aware of how quiet the streets were. How empty. She turned a full circle, slowly, her senses on high alert for reasons she could not understand. Was someone there, hidden in the shadows? Then she heard a bang – a door closing – followed by the unmistakeable sound of an engine starting, tyres screeching as it drove away in a hurry. There was a right turn up ahead which led onto Maple Lane – a long snaking road lined with town houses. It must be someone who lived there, Alex thought. Maybe they were late for work and had driven away in a hurry.

She turned and ran back towards her apartment, faster than was comfortable, her chest still tight and a feeling she couldn't shake implanted firmly in her mind: a feeling that someone had been following her.

When she arrived home she showered and made herself a coffee, piling sugar in which she hoped would provide her with enough energy to get through the day. The thought of going back to work seemed almost impossible; how could she fake it for such a long stretch of time?

She hoped it would be a distraction but she wasn't convinced that was possible – nothing could make her feel better, nothing could distract her. Her phone buzzed, reminding her of another hole she'd dug for herself: it was Henry.

> Morning. How are you?

Henry had text her several times since that night. To begin with, it was a simple *Hi, how are you feeling?* followed by a couple of question marks the following day. Then he'd tried calling one evening just as she'd opened a bottle of wine. She'd run to retrieve her phone only to be disappointed when she saw who it was. She'd silenced the call and placed the phone face down on the kitchen worktop.

There had been a couple of other texts since but they'd started to dwindle, so she was surprised and not exactly pleased to see his name on her phone now. She felt bad for ignoring him but she couldn't help feeling angry every time she saw his name flash up on her phone instead of Ryan's.

Ryan had left her apartment just before nine on Thursday night. There'd been an awkward moment at the door where neither of them had known what to do. He'd settled for a quick grasp of her hand and a sad smile; a goodbye that seemed to stall in his throat.

She'd put on a brave face and smiled back as he'd left, but the tears had come the second the door closed; quietly at first, afraid that he'd hear, then louder as the sound of his car disappeared towards the main road. She'd sobbed until sleep took her into a comfortable numbness, only to throw her from its grasp in the early hours of the morning, alone on the sofa, her hair stuck to the trails left by her tears.

———

'You all right?' Chloe passed her a mug of coffee then perched on a table opposite, her skin tanned by the coastal air. Alex was struck by the comparison: Chloe fresh-faced from two weeks off; Alex pale and exhausted. She could see concern brimming in Chloe's eyes.

'Yes, just tired. I couldn't sleep last night.'

'Monday blues?'

'Maybe. Did you have a nice break?'

'We did, thanks.' Alex couldn't help but notice the *we*, as though Chloe had used it deliberately to emphasise the fact that she was part of a *we* – a family; not just an *I* like Alex.

Chloe walked over to the window and peered out of the blinds. 'I'm sure they get earlier.'

Alex checked her watch. 'It's almost nine.' She'd been thinking about Ryan all morning – about the fact that she would have to see him dropping Mia off at school and pretend she was okay. Alex had tried to make the best of herself, she'd done her hair and make-up and put on a simple white blouse with cream trousers, but she knew the scars ran deeper than the surface. It's why she'd avoided Carol – she would take one look in her eyes and know that something was wrong. She took a big gulp of her coffee then went to open the door.

The children had already begun to form a queue, book bags and bottles of water in their hands and eager expressions on their faces. Parents gathered behind them, some talking in groups and others clearly in a hurry to get away. Alex's eyes scanned their faces and noticed Ryan at the back, his eyes fixed on Mia who was in the middle of the queue.

'Morning, everyone!' Alex did her best to sound chirpy but, hearing herself talk, she thought she'd overcompensated. 'Welcome back!' She opened the gate and the children walked up the ramp towards Chloe, excited chatter filling the air. Alex smiled as they passed but it felt unnatural and awkward and she realised it was probably the first time she'd smiled in a while; it was as though her cheeks were no longer used to the pressure and were pushing back in protest.

She waited to chat to the parents who were trying to get her attention, her eyes focused on anyone but Ryan. She couldn't work out whether he'd left yet, so she carried on talking to Finley's mum about his wobbly tooth and to Freddie's mum about his school dinners – anything to distract her from the fact that Ryan may or may not be there in the background.

When the last child was inside, she closed the gate and let her eyes sweep the playground, hoping he was there while hoping he wasn't. With a lurch to her stomach she saw he'd gone. She took a deep breath, admonishing herself for ever expecting anything else.

'Have you had any response from the parents about Friday?' Chloe was gathering the children on the carpet ready for registration and Alex got the sense she understood she wasn't on form, gently leading where usually Alex would.

'Sorry?'

'For the nature walk to the woods?'

Shit, thought Alex, she'd forgot to send out the message. They'd done the risk assessment weeks ago and decided that, for their group of twenty-eight students, they would need at least four parent volunteers. Alex and Chloe would have their own group of four, then one of the other teaching assistants, Miss McKay, would accompany them and have her own group, but that would still leave sixteen children.

Usually, Alex would have sent out a message via the school portal the previous week asking for parents to assist with the walk. There was usually a positive response from eager parents willing to help, but she'd left little time for them to sort out their work schedules or childcare arrangements for younger siblings.

'I...I...' She couldn't bring herself to tell Chloe that she'd forgotten. Usually she was so organised when it came to this sort of thing.

'I tell you what, why don't you do the register and I'll go and ask Tess to send out a quick message to the parents? We need to send a reminder out anyway.' Chloe smiled sympathetically. Alex wanted to hug her, to tell her she was sorry and that she was thankful and embarrassed and appreciative, and all of the other things which flooded her. But she couldn't, because she knew that once she opened up she wouldn't be able to stop.

'Yes, please, that would be great.'

———

Alex needn't have worried about the delay in getting the message out to parents. That afternoon, she had five people come forward and offer to help – the only problem was that Hannah was one of them.

'I can help with the trip,' she said. Her tone was clipped and Alex noticed she wasn't smiling, her eyes narrow and her jaw set. Alex's mind went into overdrive: was she angry? Did she know?

'You know what, I actually already have enough volunteers but thank you, Mrs Blake.' Alex tried to sound chirpy but the shakiness in her voice deceived her. She swallowed hard, wondering if Hannah had noticed.

'Actually, one of us should be with her anyway, because of her arm.' Hannah was clasping Mia's hand – on the other side, Mia's arm was in a white cast. Some of her friends had penned messages on it and drawn little pictures. Alex had noticed that Ryan had done the same – Daddy with a little love heart in blue ink.

'Oh, of course.' Alex fixed her eyes on Mia because she couldn't bring herself to look at Hannah. It was an odd sensation, knowing that she was the one who had wronged Hannah yet feeling as though it was the other way around. She felt a bitterness that defied logic, a fire in her chest that she was sure Hannah would feel, the flames raging, consuming everything near. 'Well, more the merrier!'

Hannah smiled but it was fleeting, there to punctuate the end of their conversation rather than anything else. Alex watched her leave, Mia skipping along beside her. Alex searched for an explanation, something to account for Hannah's hostility – something other than the fact that she'd found out about the affair. Surely, if she really did know, she would have *said* something. But then – maybe she was waiting for proof. Or for another time, when her daughter wasn't there.

Alex put her hands to her face and rubbed at her eyes, trying to calm her racing thoughts. The uneasy feeling from the morning had implanted itself deep under her skin. She swallowed down the bitter taste in her mouth and headed back into the classroom, taking one last look over her shoulder to check that Hannah had gone.

CHAPTER TWENTY-ONE

On the morning of the school trip Alex woke early. She pulled on her running kit and made her way downstairs, her eyes still heavy with sleep; she'd had a restless night and had woken with anxiety coursing through her veins. She needed to try to burn it off, to displace it before seeing Hannah.

Alex's feet pounded the pavements as she found her stride, the thick cloud hampering the sunrise, reducing it to an orange strip on the horizon. It had rained overnight and the roads were peppered with puddles, their drab greyness reflecting the heavy skies above. It was supposed to clear – she'd checked the weather forecast the previous night – but she'd sent out a reminder anyway: *Please remember wellies and rain coats, just in case!*

As she was running back towards home, a light rain dampening her skin, she became aware of a car behind her. She'd heard it approaching and thought nothing of it at first, until it slowed then continued at a crawl. She carried on running, telling herself that she was just on edge. Maybe the driver was answering a call or turning in to one of the driveways that lined the main road.

She tried to resist looking over her shoulder, focusing instead on the road ahead, but the car continued to stick behind her; she could hear the engine ticking over, the tyres moving slowly, disturbing the surface water.

A minute passed before she looked: fifty metres or so behind her, a grey hatchback was driving close to the curb, its speed reduced to almost a standstill. The headlights were off despite the dark morning, so Alex had to strain to see inside before turning back around. She could make out a shadowy silhouette behind the wheel, but that was all. What were they doing? Why were they going so slowly? There were no other cars on the road and no obstructions that she could see.

She whipped her head round again, hoping to distinguish more details – a number plate or the make of the car – but as she did, the driver floored it, rushing past her and sending rainwater spraying from the road up onto Alex's legs.

She increased her speed, running back towards her apartment with an urgency she told herself wasn't required: there were numerous reasons a car might slow in the road, she was just jittery because of all the emotion of recent weeks.

And it was a common car – dark and unremarkable – not necessarily the same one she'd seen before. Still, as she unlocked the door at the front of the building, she found herself checking over her shoulder, ensuring that the grey hatchback hadn't followed her home.

———

Alex arrived at work early. Tess, the school secretary, was already in the office, a thick pink cardigan matching a shiny gloss of lipstick.

'Good morning!' She sounded so bright and chirpy that Alex felt herself having to shift gear, to rally all her cheeriness to try to match Tess's.

'Morning!'

'I hope this weather soon clears up for your trip.'

Alex looked over to the window behind Tess. 'It seems to be drying up now.'

'Oh, that reminds me...' She stopped typing and pushed back her chair, grabbing a piece of paper from a noticeboard on the wall. 'Mia's mum called. She can't make the trip but Mr Blake's going to come instead.'

'Ryan?' Alex's hand almost shot up to her mouth, to stop herself from saying anything further. She could hear the shock in her voice, and she knew that Tess had heard it too.

'Yes... Mr Blake. Is that a problem?' Her forehead creased, her eyes narrowing.

'Oh, no, not at all.' Alex tried to laugh but it sounded almost maniacal. 'It's just... well, I hadn't expected him, that's all.' It was a poor attempt at digging herself out of a hole.

'Shame about Mrs Blake; she sounded quite upset about it.'

'Yes.' Alex wrung her hands together, suddenly aware that Tess was watching her. *Really* watching her. 'Has she been called into work?'

'I'm not sure. I didn't speak to her; she left a message – really early, actually.' She looked at the piece of paper in her hand. 'Just before six.'

'That *is* early.' Alex thought back to a few hours ago – rolling over in bed and checking the time on her phone, seeing that it was just before 5.30. Then, forty minutes later, arriving home from her run, feeling that someone had been out there – watching. Could it have been Hannah? Or was she being paranoid, piecing things together that didn't belong?

'Well...' Tess cleared her throat – Alex had been staring straight through her, her mind wandering. 'I hope you all have a lovely day today.'

Alex smiled, trying to regain her composure. 'I'm sure we will, the children are so excited. I'm going to make a drink, would you like one?' Alex was speaking too quickly, trying too hard to act casual.

Tess moved her chair back to her desk and picked up a cup of tea from next to her computer. 'I've already got one, but thanks.'

'No problem! Have a good day!' As she walked away, Alex felt an odd prickling sensation gathering at the base of her neck; she felt sure it was Tess's eyes, searching for what Alex knew had to remain hidden.

———

Ryan hovered at the back of the classroom while Alex and Chloe set about trying to ensure all the children were ready and everything was packed. He was wearing jeans and a black Nike hoody and stood with his jaw set and his hands in his pockets. If she didn't know him better she'd think he seemed unapproachable and arrogant, his eyes fixed on a spot on the floor and his mouth showing no trace of a smile. It was as though he didn't want to be here, she thought, before realising that was exactly what it was.

'I've got the first aid kit.' Chloe held up a green bag before stuffing it into her backpack. 'Have you got the register?'

'Yep, it's here.' Alex showed her a blue clipboard before slipping into her coat. The rain had stopped but it still looked temperamental outside, the day never having brightened, hindered by the low cloud which seemed to fall in a hazy mist of grey. 'Right, class!' she shouted. 'Is everyone ready?'

There was a communal 'yes' from the children as the parents stood eagerly awaiting instruction.

'Right, we have Finley's mum, Mrs Daniels...' Finley stood smiling by his mother's side. 'Joining you will be Rio, Jessica and Violet.' Alex read out the groups for the other parents, reeling off names as she usually would without a second thought, until she came to Ryan. Her hands trembled as she clutched the clipboard and she felt flustered and self-conscious in a way that made her fidgety, her feet shuffling on the floor as she repeatedly tucked her hair behind her ears.

She put extra energy into trying to sound flippant but her voice was betraying her, catching in her throat as though objecting to saying his name. 'Mr Blake, you have Mia and Orla with you today.' She quickly shifted her focus to Chloe and Miss McKay, handing out a list of which children were with which adult. Once they were all ready to go, Alex propped open the door and led everyone outside.

The coolness bit at her cheeks, the winds lifting the ends of her hair. She breathed deeply, thankful to be outside where she felt the awkwardness easing slightly, drifting into the breeze. The space outside afforded her the opportunity to gather herself in a way which felt impossible inside, contained in the same room as Ryan.

They walked down Field Street in a long line, the children wearing their high-vis vests over their coats, then they turned right onto Beck Lane. The trees on either side clambered towards each other, their limbs touching at the top. There was no traffic there aside from the odd car from the residents, and she felt the adults relax, the comparable safety of the wider, quieter paths a relief.

The woodland loomed up ahead, her childhood home sat off to the side of it, the end of the long driveway just visible beside the treeline. Her group of children walked beside her in pairs, holding hands and chatting happily, pointing out the birds which dived into the fields beside them looking for food among the undergrowth.

Alex had barely spoken. Usually, she would be pointing out the nature that surrounded them, commenting on the weather or the horses in the field up ahead, but she didn't have the energy or enthusiasm. They reached an opening in the treeline and Alex stopped and waited for everyone to catch up.

'I'll just do a quick head count.' She moved between the groups making sure she counted each child. As she passed Ryan she kept her eyes down, focusing on Mia and Orla who were stood beside him. Her skin prickled, his effect on her no less intoxicating despite his detachment. She felt angry. How could he be so cold? And why was she still lusting after him, her heart controlling her head? She knew he wasn't a bad person: he must be in self-preservation mode, soldiering through in order to get to the other side – a side where his feelings for Alex no longer existed. But knowing he wasn't a bad person didn't make her any less angry or hurt. In fact, it felt worse. She wanted to hate him. It would be so much easier.

'Twenty-seven… twenty-eight. Okay, everyone's here, let's go!' She led everyone into the woodland, Alex at the front and Miss McKay at the back. She took the main footpath, skirting the stream before coming out at the grassy area – the secret garden. The last time she was there she'd been invited to Edward and Rosemary's barbeque. She shook her head, trying to physically dislodge the memories from her mind.

'Okay, we'll stop here and do some exploring in our little groups.' She took out some sheets of paper and handed them out to each of the children. 'There are some things listed on here which I think you'll be able to find here in the woodland. We can search under logs and rocks but *please*,' she paused for emphasis, 'be careful and respectful to the woodland.' She checked the time on her watch then addressed the adults. 'We'll meet back here in forty-five minutes to chat about what we've found, okay?'

The groups dispersed, some children flocking to the treeline while others held back. Alex had four children with her – Logan, Isla, Freddie and Sienna. Freddie was pulling Logan's arm, trying to get him to take a narrow path to the left where a tree had fallen down years before and now sat rotting on its side.

'That's a good idea, Freddie, lots of animals like damp dark spaces. Let's go and look.'

They disappeared between the trees and Alex followed, the ground soft beneath her boots and the wind hissing through the leafy canopy above, fragments of sky visible between the green. Alex could hear the rushing of the stream ahead and, piercing through it, the sound of laughter. She ducked out of the way of a low-hanging branch and as she stood she realised they weren't alone. Mia and Orla were lifting a rock and Logan had run over to help.

'Mia, be careful,' she heard Ryan saying, then, as he saw Alex appear: 'Oh, hi, Miss Vaughn.'

'We found worms!' Mia laughed.

'Let me see!' Isla skipped over to the rock while Sienna prodded the rotting tree with a stick.

Alex smiled but didn't say anything. The children all gravitated towards each other, exchanging ideas and investigating the muddy earth around them. Ryan stood back and watched and Alex noticed he'd drifted towards her.

'I'm sorry I'm here. It wasn't my idea.'

'No need to apologise.'

'I couldn't really say no, what with Mia's arm.'

'I understand. It's fine.'

She heard him exhale heavily beside her but her eyes remained on the children, her hands clutching the clipboard.

'This is… difficult,' he said quietly. She could feel his eyes on her and she wasn't sure whether to turn and meet his gaze or gather up her group and run away from it. In the end, her heart won, as she feared it always would. She turned to face him and being closer she noticed his bloodshot eyes and the grey half-circles underneath them. She wanted to reach out and hold him, to comfort him in the same way she wanted to be comforted herself.

'Yes, it is.'

'I think about you all the time.' His voice was low and she had to move closer to him to hear.

'Don't. Don't say that.'

'It's true.'

'Ryan, you ended things. You have to let me move on.'

'I ended things because... because...' he stammered, his fingers pinching the bridge of his nose. He looked over his shoulder then back to her. 'Come here a sec.' He gestured towards a copse of trees, their trunks growing so close to each other that there was little room between them.

Alex looked at the children playing happily, oblivious to what was going on between her and Ryan. Mia was sat on a rock, Freddie and Logan gathering pebbles which they were arranging into a pile at her feet.

Alex knew she shouldn't leave them, even for a second, but it was a matter of metres and she would be able to hear them if anything happened. Ryan turned towards the trees and, after a moment's hesitation, Alex followed.

CHAPTER TWENTY-TWO

Ryan stopped suddenly and turned to face her, less than ten metres from the group of children they'd left beyond the trees. Alex could still hear their chatter; the occasional excitable squeal. It reassured her.

'This is driving me mad.' He scratched his head then rubbed his hand across his face. He looked forlorn in the same way she felt and she couldn't help but feel comforted – he was hurting too. It confirmed to her that what they'd shared was real – it wasn't one-sided or an exaggeration as she'd began to fear. 'I've never felt like this before. It feels…'

'Impossible?' Alex offered.

'Yeah. Impossible.' He stepped towards her, narrowing the gap she'd purposefully left. 'I don't think I can do this, I can't function without you. I'm going insane, I'm making mistakes at work… I can't sleep… I can't focus on anything.'

Alex took a deep breath, trying to think straight. She didn't want to act on impulse, to melt back into his arms, despite every fibre of her body wanting exactly that. She needed to safeguard herself.

'Ryan, I can't do this whole on-again off-again thing. I can't be sat around waiting to hear from you, staying home in case you turn up… that's no life.'

'I know, I know. Look, can we talk? Properly, I mean.' There was an urgency to his words and a plea to his tone which Alex couldn't ignore. Behind her, Alex could hear a child laughing. 'I could come round to yours and we could talk about it without any distractions?'

'I don't see what there is to say. You're married. I'm not.' She swallowed hard, trying to suppress what she knew was hope; a naïve and anticipative hope. She had to quash it, she was getting ahead of herself – he wasn't going to leave Hannah, was he?

'There has to be a way… there has to be something we can do to make this work.'

'Ryan,' she said, her tone firm. 'I thought I could accept having part of you, but I've realised I can't. It's not enough. You said you want me to be ha–'

'I do.'

'But this,' she gestured between the two of them. 'This isn't making me happy. When I'm with you, I'm happy, but when you've gone back to your wife and your child and I'm left on my own… I've never felt so alone.'

He rubbed at his eyes with his fingertips and when he looked at her again she noticed that the blueness of them seemed to have faded, dulled by the emotional turmoil of the last couple of weeks. Or by the lies. 'I want to talk properly, there are things you don't know.'

'What things?'

'I can't talk about it here, Alex.' His eyes glanced over her shoulder, beyond the trees where his daughter played. 'Please, let me come round so we can talk about this?'

'I don't know if that's a good idea.'

Before she knew what was happening he'd taken her hand in his, his body so close she could feel his warmth. He kissed her gently on her cheek, the stubble on his chin rough against her skin. She didn't look up at him, she couldn't – she knew where that would lead. He put his finger under her chin and gently tilted her head up to face him, then he bent down and kissed her.

She wanted to stop him, to step back and tell him she couldn't go down this road again, but time seemed to pass by without her noticing. She heard the snap of twigs behind her and a bird singing above – it pulled her gently back to the present, but slowly and without urgency. Eventually she stepped back.

'We can't do this here, Ryan.'

'I know. I know.' He was smiling, his blue, blue eyes reignited. She couldn't help but smile back. 'I'm sorry. Can I see you tonight?'

But before she could answer they were interrupted by a noise, one which Alex couldn't place at first. It sounded almost animal-like – piercing and primal. A couple of birds above them took flight in response, but Alex didn't move. An eerie silence followed the scream. Alex and Ryan looked at each other, frozen, encircled by the thicket of trees; surrounded by their protection, she wouldn't have to face what lay beyond.

She felt her senses heighten, her ears picking up the rustle of the leaves above; the distant call of a bird; the murmur of the wind weaving through the woodland; an aeroplane descending somewhere out in a world which she suddenly felt so far removed from. But more than anything, she could hear what was absent – the silence left by the children.

Alex was holding her breath, afraid to move or make a sound. Then, suddenly, life continued. Ryan leapt forward – a burst of movement and noise as he ran through the forest. Alex turned slowly at first, following him with her eyes, before the adrenaline surged into her limbs, forcing her to act.

Then she was gone too, following the same path as Ryan, towards the scream that had temporarily suspended everything. She felt the wilderness snag at her clothes and pull at her hair as though trying to hold her back, her boots sliding against the damp earth below. It took a matter of seconds to reach the point where they'd stood before, but so much had gone through Alex's mind in that time – flashes of information, of what-ifs and maybes. What if someone was hurt? What if people found out she'd left them unsupervised? What if they'd been taken?

When she arrived back in the little clearing with the long-forgotten tree and the upturned rocks she stopped, searching the area with quick turns of her head. She could hear a commotion beyond the place that had seemed so safe only moments before, noises she could tell came from more than just the children that had been there.

She stepped over the rotting wood, between a couple of silver birch trees and back onto the gravelly path which led to the stream. She ran towards the noise despite wanting to run away from it, despite knowing that whatever she found there wouldn't be good. She could see a blur of colour between the shrubs, flashes of pink and blue and yellow, the multi-coloured coats of the children with the high-vis vests over the top.

She emerged at the bank, her breathing erratic and her eyes wild with horror. By the edge of the water she could see movement. A man, knelt down, something in his hands obscured by the reedy undergrowth. She edged closer. It was Ryan and, in his arms, Mia, the blood that covered her face a stark contrast to the paleness of her skin.

CHAPTER TWENTY-THREE

Hannah burst into the school at fifteen minutes to nine on Monday morning, just over a week after the school trip. Alex was waiting in the staffroom – she was due to have a meeting with the head teacher, though she already had her notice typed out in her handbag.

She was clutching her bag close to her side when, in the hallway, she heard Tess's voice. She sounded flustered, her voice getting louder as she grew nearer.

'I'm sorry, she barged in, I couldn't stop her...'

'Where is she?' Hannah shouted. 'Where is she?'

'Mrs Blake, I understand you're upset but you can't just...' Mrs Harlow, the head teacher, was trying to employ her firm-but-fair voice but she'd clearly been caught off guard.

The door to the staffroom flung open and bounced off the wall. Hannah pushed it back again, her eyes wide and wild, glaring at Alex.

'You sly little bitch!' She looked as though she'd been crying, her skin was pale and blotchy and her eyes swollen and red. Behind her, Mrs Harlow and Tess stood in the doorway looking aghast.

'Mrs Blake...' Alex began. 'Hannah... I'm so sorry about Mia...'

'Don't you dare!'

'Mrs Blake, please, if we could just–' Mrs Harlow tried, but Hannah ignored her, speaking over her as though she wasn't there.

'How long's it been going on?' Hannah asked. 'How long?'

Other members of staff appeared out in the hallway looking for the source of the commotion. Some craned their necks to see inside, others tiptoed to see over the heads of those already there. Alex wanted to shout at them, she wanted to tell them to go – this was not a show. This was her *life*.

'I don't know what you mean...' Alex began, but she knew her denials were futile. Hannah knew about her and Ryan, and soon everyone else would too.

'How long have you been *fucking* my husband?'

Mrs Harlow stepped between them and Alex noticed her expression had changed to one of horror as the realisation dawned. 'Please, Mrs Blake, there are children outside.'

'Han... Hannah... where is she?' Alex could hear a voice. Male. It took her a few seconds to realise it was Ryan, his voice panicked. He appeared in the doorway and pushed past the people who were gathered there. 'Hannah, Mia's upset. Don't do this, not here.'

'Don't you dare tell me what to do! If you cared so much about Mia you wouldn't have been screwing her teacher!'

Ryan looked mortified, his eyes darting around the room, taking in the expressions of shock on the faces of everyone watching. Alex wanted to go to him, to put her arms around him and comfort him in the way she wanted to be comforted. To tell him everything would be okay even though she knew that wasn't the truth. She longed to be alone with him, for everyone else to simply cease to exist.

'Right, everyone else, leave,' Mrs Harlow shouted, ushering

everyone away and closing the door. 'Mr and Mrs Blake, if you would like to file a formal complaint then–'

Ryan interrupted. 'No, we don't want to do that.' He turned to face Hannah. 'Han, you know things haven't been good – that doesn't excuse what I did but we need to talk about this as a couple. Not here.'

Alex felt the pain in her heart as though he'd stabbed her right in it, a searing white-hot sting which lingered long after his words. She put her hand to her chest as though afraid something would fall out if she didn't. Seeing Ryan go to Hannah instead of her was exactly what she knew would happen yet everything she hoped wouldn't. She wanted to be his priority. She wanted to be the one that he went to. Instead, he placed his hand on Hannah's arm as though waiting to usher her from the room.

When he spoke again his voice was quiet but firm. 'I'm not the only one who's lied.'

'Don't you dare...' She snatched her arm away but the anger in her voice had softened. Whatever implication had been in Ryan's words, it had worked.

Ryan turned to Mrs Harlow. 'Mia's coming in with Orla. I'm sorry about all this. Let's go, Han. Please.'

Hannah stood with watery eyes, the anger subsiding long enough for Alex to glimpse the raw devastation. Then Hannah took one last look at Alex before storming back out of the room, the door slamming against the wall, Ryan following dutifully in her wake.

———

Almost three months passed in a dream-like state – a *nightmare*-like state – time moving in a bizarre way that made her feel unmoored. Sometimes an hour would pass unbearably slowly, filled with the crippling weight of guilt; other times, a week would fly by in a blur and Alex wouldn't be able to recall the days which filled it.

She'd been exhausted for weeks, a crippling fatigue that had induced long dreamless sleeps. The nausea had come a few weeks later. She told herself it was the anxiety – the emotional toll the accident had taken on her had been intolerable – but even in the early days she knew it was something more than that. She retreated into the relative safety of denial, knowing that admitting the reality of her situation would open wounds which had not yet had chance to heal.

But this wasn't something that would disappear. This wasn't something she could hide or pretend didn't exist. This was about more than her. More than Ryan. She looked at the plastic test in her hand and the two crystal clear lines that had appeared on the screen, perfect yet fragile. She realised she could no longer hide away, sheltering herself from the things she needed to do.

Alex had spent the last few weeks knowing that she was pregnant while refusing to believe it. Some part of her mind had pieced things together which Alex didn't want to see, so she'd continued to avert her gaze, refusing to think about it. She'd felt oddly detached from it, as though she was watching it all unfold in someone else's life.

She'd managed to keep up the pretence through the usual list of pregnancy symptoms but now, for some reason, she could no longer refuse to give it space. It had leapt to the forefront of her mind and demanded to be heard. The test was the alarming and undisputable proof she needed. She sat on the single bed in her old bedroom with it clutched in her hand, hardly daring to imagine her future.

She'd moved back to her parents' house a couple of weeks before. She'd let her apartment go for much less than the estate agent had insisted it was worth, needing to be free from the things which bound her. It was a temporary arrangement, moving back in with her parents – transitional – though she wasn't sure yet exactly what she would be transitioning to. Or where.

The curtains were closed but a narrow streak of the afternoon sun found its way in through the gap in the middle, lighting up the dusky pink carpet and stretching out towards her unmade bed. She watched as little dust particles danced in its glow. She'd taken to sleeping most of the day, plagued by memories of what had happened and dread of what was yet to come.

After the accident, Mia had been taken to hospital and the rest of the children back to school. Parents were called. Questions were asked. An internal investigation ensued. Alex and Ryan had both had to provide statements, along with every other adult who was there. Mia had ended up with a glued eyebrow and steri-strips to help heal the laceration she'd got when she fell. The children had wandered out of the clearing chasing a butterfly. Mia had balanced on a rock – ineffectively on account of her broken arm – and she'd fallen hard onto the jagged edge of it.

Chloe had taken charge; she'd assumed the children had wandered off just ahead of Alex and Ryan, running while the adults walked. She hadn't for a second doubted Alex's capabilities, so this was the narrative Alex and Ryan silently agreed to and the one they delivered in their statements – the children had skipped off ahead and Mia had fallen. The delay in reaching them was due to the slippery ground.

The accident alone might have been accepted as exactly that in the community – a terrible mishap, Alex completely blameless – if it weren't for Hannah finding out about the affair, and subsequently making sure everyone else knew about it too. How quickly it had all been swept away. One minute, the hope had risen as she clutched on to the words of the man she loved. And the next, it had all been shattered, along with everything else.

Alex had felt like a complete failure. The shame and humiliation had seeped out from within so that they became a physical presence, something she wore for all to see. She'd neglected her pupils, and one of them was harmed as a result. Alex knew she'd crossed a line that had put an end to her career – how could she ever trust herself again? How could she ever feel capable and responsible? She'd prided herself on her dedication, her professionalism, and all it had taken for her to forget over a decade of good practice was for one man to turn her head.

Alex closed her eyes, the test still clutched in her hand. She could not ignore this any longer. She took her phone off the nightstand and typed out a message.

I need to see you.

CHAPTER TWENTY-FOUR

She waited until the narrow strip of sunlight had faded; until her mum had been in to try to encourage her to go down for dinner; until she'd been in again with a bowl of beef stew and a cup of tea balanced on a tray. He'd read the message – she could see from the blue tick – but he hadn't replied.

She considered trying to call him but she was afraid that Hannah would answer – perhaps she was monitoring his phone, suspicion replacing trust. Alex couldn't go round to his house and she couldn't contact him via email or social media, so she was left with little choice. She picked up her phone and typed out another message.

> This is bigger than us, Ryan. I need to see you.

This time he replied straight away.

> I can't. I'm sorry.

Heat prickled in her eyes but she blinked the tears away – it was not the time for her emotions to rule, she needed to keep a clear head, to be strong.

> Either you come to me, or I'll have to come to you.

She saw him typing, then stopping, then typing again, repeating the same pattern for the next couple of minutes until finally, he responded.

> Meet me at the entrance to the woods in an hour. I can't stay long.

———

'I'm going for a walk.'

Carol looked at her sceptically but chose not to voice her concerns – the long list of them that she'd collected over the past couple of months and hidden away, concealed by everything but her eyes; they seemed cloudy, heavy with disquiet.

Alex felt a pang of guilt whenever she looked at her. Out of everything she'd had to endure, the thing she'd found most difficult to swallow was the way her mum had been treated as a result of *her* failings. That had seemed particularly unfair to Alex, though her mum had of course tried to hide the impact. *It doesn't matter, Alex, don't you worry about me, I'll be fine.*

She was no longer welcome at her walking group. She'd been shunned by the local community. She was, once more, an outcast through no fault of her own, and this pained Alex – it broke through the numbness like a rush of fire.

Alex knew she'd not been easy to live with, her emotions up and down and her tendency to retreat into her room a constant feature. She'd been unable to accept her mum's help quite simply because she didn't feel as though she deserved it. Carol had been gentle in her response, always making herself available to her but never pushing too hard. Alex wanted to tell her how thankful she was but she was afraid that once she let her guard down she wouldn't be able to pick herself back up.

If her mum had been shocked by the news of her affair she hadn't let it show. If she'd thought it was humiliating or shameful, she'd managed to keep it to herself, choosing instead to tell Alex that everyone makes mistakes. Hannah had taken it upon herself to make sure that every single person in Elwood knew what had happened between Alex and Ryan. She'd told everyone how Mia had seen Daddy hugging and kissing Miss Vaughn in the woods on the school trip; that she'd asked Hannah quite innocently why they were such good friends.

She'd told everyone about the messages she'd later found on Ryan's phone under 'Alex Work'. And she'd told everyone how their little rendezvous in the woods had been the reason that Mia had needed to go to hospital; the reason she would likely have a scar for the rest of her life. Hannah said things like 'neglectful' and 'incompetent' – words that Alex had called herself hundreds of times, but seemed incomprehensibly worse coming from others.

Alex had been a much-loved teacher at the school and her roots in Elwood had elevated her to a position of respect in the wider community. The fall from grace had been fast and ruthless. Small communities stuck together. Alex was now an outsider, and by extension of her wrongdoings, so were her parents. Alex knew her mum had stopped going to the walking group, and when she asked her why she'd become flustered, telling her it wasn't really her thing anyway.

'Are they saying stuff about me, Mum?'

'Oh, Alex, don't worry about what people round here say.'

Alex put on her trainers and unlocked the door. Carol hovered in the hallway in her nightie – white with delicate pink flowers. Alex wondered how long she'd had it; she could remember being a little girl and crawling into her mum's bed while her dad was away – Carol was wearing that same nightie then.

'Do you need a torch?'

'No, I'll be fine.'

She gave Alex a thin smile before returning to the sofa to watch her TV shows.

She walked briskly to the end of the gravelly path then turned right past the woodland, stopping as she drew level with the entrance. An orange street lamp flickered weakly at the opposite side of the lane and, further down towards the junction with Field Street, she could see Mr Pratchett's bungalow sat back among the fields, the lights still on and the distant sound of his dog barking. It was a warm evening, clear skies revealing a blanket of stars. Under different circumstances, she would probably have considered it romantic. Now she felt as though they were mocking her, the stars and all their magnificence.

Ahead, she could just make out a car approaching slowly as it manoeuvred the potholed path and the dimly lit corners of Beck Lane. Her eyes narrowed, trying to get a better view. As it drew nearer, she realised it wasn't Ryan's car but a hatchback – dark in colour. It stopped beside one of the fields, the engine idling. Behind, she could make out a figure approaching. It was moving quickly – running. She watched as he drew nearer, knowing without being sure how that it was Ryan. Absent-mindedly, she drew her hand to her stomach, her palm flat against it.

A moment later, Ryan was stood in front of her. Her eyes darted to the car and Ryan followed her gaze before gesturing into the shadowy darkness of the treeline. She moved back and, as she did, she heard the car moving again. It turned awkwardly, the tyres crunching against the path, then drove away. She turned her attention back to Ryan. He was sweating, dressed in a pair of black shorts and a white T-shirt.

'Hi.' He put his hands on his hips and tried to get control of his breathing. 'Had to say I was going out for a run.'

Alex nodded. She understood. 'I'm sorry to call you out like this. I... I needed to talk to you.' He didn't say anything, just waited patiently for what she needed to tell him so urgently. Suddenly all the words she'd rehearsed before leaving the house seemed to evaporate from her mind. Instead, she wanted to ask him if it was all real and whether he was hurting as much as she was. She wanted to ask him if he missed her in the same way that she missed him – so completely that at times it was hard to breathe. But that wasn't what she was there for. She took a deep, steadying breath.

'I'm pregnant.'

Ryan's eyebrows shot up in surprise but the rest of him didn't even flinch. A moment passed, the silence thick and heavy between them. He pushed his hair away from his face then rubbed at his jawline.

'Ryan? Say something, please.'

'I don't... erm... congratulations?' It was phrased as a question rather than a comment, as though asking whether this was in fact news to be congratulated. It struck Alex as odd.

'I don't expect you to be over the moon about it but I thought you should know.'

'Right.' He looked around, over his shoulders at first and then sweeping the treeline. Alex couldn't work out whether he was thinking or whether he simply had nothing else to say, but she felt a sudden rush of disappointment. Of all the things she'd expected, this was not the way she'd wanted it to go. He seemed unfazed but in a way that screamed disinterest rather than acceptance.

'Ryan,' she pleaded. 'Please, say something. Tell me how you feel.'

'Alex, it really has nothing to do with me.'

'Nothing to do with you? You got me pregnant but it has nothing to do with you?'

'I got... sorry, what?'

'You're the father, Ryan. I thought that was obvious, why else would I be telling you?'

'I'm *not* the father.' His words were so devoid of emotion that they hurt all the more for it. More than shouting or screaming or name-calling. He seemed so cold. So distant.

'Yes, you are. I'm going to have this baby with or without your support.' Alex wasn't aware that she'd made a decision about the baby, she hadn't allowed herself to think about it enough to come to a conclusion, but hearing herself speak with such conviction she realised that there had never been a decision to make.

'Alex, I promise you: I'm not the father of your baby. It's not possible.'

'What do you mean it's not possible?'

'I can't have children.'

'But… yes you can… you have Mia.'

'She's not my biological daughter.'

'No, no, that… that can't… that can't be right.' She was raspy, her chest tight as she spoke. She began pacing, her feet shuffling back and forth against the gravelly path, the humid air clinging to her skin. Ryan took a couple of steps towards her and placed his hands on her shoulders, grounding her.

'I promise you, I can't be the father.'

She looked deep into his eyes, searching for the truth she wasn't sure she even wanted. There was such intensity in them, such sincerity and strength.

'I don't understand. I don't… I don't understand.' She felt the tears begin to fall and her voice begin to falter. She was breathless. She clutched Ryan's arms and let herself fall into him, her cheek pressing against his chest. He didn't say anything, he just held her there, one hand gently brushing the back of her head. She couldn't help but think about how she never wanted to be anywhere else.

'Have you always known?' she asked him.

'No.' He stepped back and sniffed, rubbing at his eyes with

his fingertips. 'When Mia was two we started trying for another baby. Nothing happened. After a year or so we sought help, tried to find out what was going on, you know?' Alex nodded, she did not know, but she wanted to. 'I was told I couldn't have children naturally. We could go down the IVF route but... well, I haven't exactly felt like having a baby with a woman who lied to me.' He tried to smile but it looked sad and forced and it made Alex's heart break for him. 'That's why things haven't been good between me and Han. I couldn't get my head around it.'

'I'm so sorry.'

'She'd been seeing someone else when we hooked up at that wedding, but she'd never told me about it at the time. She'd allowed me to think Mia was biologically mine.'

'Did she know?'

'That she wasn't?' He shrugged. 'I don't know what to believe anymore.' He looked up at the sky for a moment. Alex's eyes never left him. It occurred to her that his lack of genetic link to Mia was probably the thing which had tied him to Hannah, too afraid that to leave the family home would be to leave the family altogether. How unfair, Alex thought, that Hannah's lies and deceit would end up being the thing which got her everything she wanted.

Alex remembered what he'd said to her in the woods: *I just want to talk properly, there are things you don't know.* And his words to Hannah in the staffroom at school: *I'm not the only one who's lied.* It all made sense now.

'I'm still her father,' he said firmly, his eyes back on Alex. 'It makes no difference to the way I feel about Mia.'

'Of course not.' Alex was trying to be fully engaged in the conversation, to take in every word, but at the back of her mind the repercussions of what he was telling her were starting to overshadow everything else. It was like pulling on a string – at first the enormity of what it meant didn't occur to her but, as the minutes passed by and the string continued to unravel, so did everything else.

'I'm so sorry about your job. I never meant for any of this.'

'I know.'

'What will you do?'

'I'm not sure.' She didn't know whether he meant about getting a job or about the baby, but the same answer applied to both. She had no idea. About anything.

'Is it that guy's... the one I saw you with?' He gestured towards Alex's stomach, which was churning, an unsettling truth weighing heavily on her. She wanted to tell Ryan everything. She wanted to tell him that she didn't understand, that she didn't think anything had happened between her and Henry. She wanted to tell him that she wished this baby were his; that she wished *she* were his. But this wasn't Ryan's baby, and she wasn't Ryan's wife.

'I should go,' she said, the words snagging in her throat.

'I never meant to fall in love with you.' His words came out hurried and it took Alex a moment to make sense of them. 'But I did.' He swallowed hard and kicked at a stone on the ground. 'I think I always will.'

Before Alex could respond he turned and ran back the way he'd come, towards Mr Pratchett's bungalow with the lights still on and the tunnel of trees which led to the main road.

Away from her.

When he was nothing but a silhouette in the distance she whispered: 'I love you too.'

CHAPTER TWENTY-FIVE

Alex met Emma at a café in the back streets of Nottingham; large enough to ensure space to talk while being small enough not to overwhelm her. She felt vulnerable. When she'd gone outside to her car that morning, she'd found writing scrawled into the thin layer of dust that had collected across the windscreen: SLUT.

She'd looked around, suddenly on edge, but there was nothing to see but the dense treeline and the old farmhouse. Inside the car, she'd quickly turned on the wipers and watched as the letters washed away, knowing they would remain fixed in her mind. Had Hannah paid her a visit in the early hours? Or had someone else from the village taken it upon themselves to try to drive her out?

The city centre was busy and, after she'd parked her car, there was a moment of apprehension where she'd paused, questioning whether she could go through with it. She told herself she was being paranoid, imagining passers-by staring at her, whispering to friends or colleagues. It took all of her strength to put one foot in front of the other and find her way to the café.

She arrived a couple of minutes early and chose a table in the far corner, away from the heat of the sun which flooded in through a large window at the front. The table rocked as she sat down, the off-white Formica top stained with beige coffee rings. A middle-aged woman with strawberry blonde hair held her forefinger up from her position by the counter and mouthed *one sec.*

She was serving a couple of men in high-vis vests and work boots, punching buttons on the ancient looking till. The place smelled like bacon and coffee with an undertone of cheap lemon-scented cleaning products. In the centre of the table was a small white dish full of sugar cubes – a mixture of brown and white. Alex fiddled with the bowl as she waited, twirling it around with her fingers.

The door opened and Emma walked in in a flurry. Alex was surprised by how different she looked – she was used to seeing her glammed up in the evening, her hair down and lipstick on. But today she was dressed for work – smart black trousers and a sleeveless white shirt, a dainty silver necklace sitting just above the top button. Her highlighted hair was pinned back in a slick bun and she was wearing only a trace of make-up. She looked nice. Professional. It made Alex feel sad for reasons she couldn't quite put her finger on. Perhaps it was the contrast – Alex sat in her shorts and T-shirt, her hair greasy and eyes sunken and red. She let her hair fall forward, partially obscuring her face.

'Sorry, sorry,' Emma said, pulling out a chair. 'I got held up at the office. I need to order, I'm starving.' She turned round as the waitress came walking over. 'Can I get a jacket potato with cheese and a diet Coke?'

The woman scribbled her order down on a little pad before turning to Alex.

'Just a coffee, please.'

'You're not eating?'

'I'm not hungry.'

Emma's face softened and she looked for a moment to be on the edge of expressing concern, but seemed to think better of it and instead ploughed head first into a story about something that had happened at work that morning. Alex tried to nod and smile in all the right places but she was struggling to concentrate. There was a clock on the wall above the counter and her eyes kept flitting up to it, wondering how much longer Emma was going to talk for.

'So,' she said finally. 'You said you needed to talk?'

'Um, yes. I need to know about what happened that night.'

'What night?' She frowned. 'When we last went out?'

'Yeah.'

'You don't remember?'

'Not really, no. I was wasted. I know I texted Henry...' She swallowed hard and tucked her hair behind her ear. 'I know I texted him and asked him to meet me – I found the messages on my phone.'

'Yeah...'

'And I know he stayed over at mine.'

'I told you not to go with him. There was something weird about him.'

'Weird? How so?'

'Well, you text him to meet us then he appeared like thirty seconds later. No way could he have walked from The Garden Room in that time.'

'You think he was already there?'

'Definitely.'

'You think he followed us?'

Emma shrugged. 'I don't know, but he wouldn't leave you alone. Don't get me wrong, it didn't seem to bother you – especially at first, you were all over him – but it was just a bit odd.'

'In what way?'

'The way he looked at you. He had this stare, like he couldn't look away.' Emma widened her eyes and ceased blinking, demonstrating. 'Then we said our goodbyes and moved on to that bar with the cheap shots... I can't remember its name... but he turned up. He hovered in the distance, watching you.'

Alex felt her skin tingling. She couldn't remember any of it.

'You're sure?'

'I'm sure. I was tipsy but I was nowhere near as drunk as you. In fact, I've never seen you like that before.'

'I hadn't eaten much...'

'Yeah but do we ever on a night out?'

Alex didn't reply, she was desperately trying to get her brain to clutch on to something Emma had told her, to unlock the memories she didn't seem to have access to.

'Anyway, later on that night I was trying to put you in a cab and that Henry guy turns up and insists on going with you. He said he lived nearby and he would drop you off first, check you got home okay.'

Alex wanted to scream. She was suddenly filled with rage. How could Emma have let her go home with a stranger when she was that drunk? It went against every code in the book. Emma must have noticed the fury in Alex's eyes; she cleared her throat and lowered her voice.

'Alex, did something happen?'

Tears were falling down her cheeks. Sad, angry tears full of disbelief. They fell to her lips and she licked away the saltiness, wiping the rest on the back of her hand. She could not remember anything, no matter how much she tried. It was like a black hole.

'I tried to tell you not to go with him.' Emma reached across the table and took Alex's hand. 'I asked you to come to mine but you kept insisting. You said you knew him through work. I thought maybe he was the guy you'd told me about.' She looked around and lowered her voice to a whisper. 'The *married* one.'

Alex shook her head almost imperceptibly.

'Alex, what's wrong? What can I do?'

The waitress appeared next to them, a tray in her hands balancing a mug of coffee and a glass of diet Coke. She placed them on the table but, noticing Alex's tears, hurried away without saying a word.

'Nothing,' Alex whispered. 'There's nothing you can do.'

———

Alex traipsed around the city in a daze. Emma had offered to take the afternoon off work to stay with her but Alex had refused. She wanted to be alone. Actually, she wanted to be with Ryan, but being alone was the next best thing. Emma hadn't pressed for information – maybe she didn't want to have her morals as a friend questioned by the consequences of that night. People were funny like that – the things that were left unspoken were easier to hide from, despite the glaring and obvious reality of what went unsaid.

Alex left when Emma's food arrived, making her excuses and leaving without telling her about the pregnancy. She couldn't bear to utter the words and she felt that, out of all the people she could tell, Emma was somewhere near the bottom of the list. Alex couldn't decide if her anger towards her was warranted, but it certainly felt it.

She sat down on some steps at the Old Market Square, the city alive with the buzz of lunchtime. The fountains were on and a couple of children had taken off their shoes and socks and were paddling in the water, their parents or grandparents hovering nearby. A man in a suit came and sat on the steps behind Alex, a baguette and a newspaper in his hands. People surrounded her, everyone going about their day, oblivious to the knot tightening in her stomach. She took her phone out of her bag and scrolled through the contacts. Among them, she found what she was looking for. *Henry – may or may not call.*

She looked at his name for a while, trying to remember the day they'd met on the training course. She had a vague image of him wearing a checked shirt with a jumper over the top and a pair of wire-framed glasses. He'd seemed confident yet jittery, from what she could remember – confident as he spoke in a professional capacity but suddenly nervous when the topic had veered away.

He'd sat next to her as they'd been tasked with reading a case study and delivering a response to it. He'd tentatively asked her where she worked and made other small talk she could not recall, but she'd never got the impression that it was anything more than politeness. The skin on her neck prickled and she shuddered. The thought of something happening between them when she was so catastrophically drunk repulsed her.

She looked at the text she'd sent him the night they met at The Garden Room: *Come to V Lounge!* It was the only message Alex had sent him. Following that, there were a chain of messages from Henry:

Hi, how are you feeling?

Hi, I just called to see how you are? Henry.

Fancy that drink?

Hope you're having a good week!

Morning. How are you?

She hadn't replied to any of them. She thought back to the morning after, to Henry standing at her bedroom door looking bashful at her level of undress. *I was going to leave but you kept asking me to stay, so I slept on the sofa.* She'd assumed she'd passed out drunk in bed and he'd hunkered down for a night on the sofa. Had something occurred before?

She typed out a message on her phone.

> Hi, Henry. Fancy a coffee tomorrow? Meet you in Nottingham?

She pressed send, swallowing down the overwhelming urge to be sick.

CHAPTER TWENTY-SIX

Henry had text back within minutes telling her he would be free in the afternoon. She replied telling him she would meet him by the fountains at one and he'd responded with a thumbs up emoji and said that he would bring the coffees. Alex had showered early then had breakfast with her mum – something she'd previously been avoiding. The act of sitting across the table from a woman who could read her better than anyone scared her.

She'd been sure that she would take one look in her eyes and see she was pregnant. Logic told her that eventually she would *have* to tell her but, for the time being, she couldn't. She needed to get things straight in her head, to clear away the fog so that she could decide what to do. She knew she was going to keep the baby, but everything else felt so uncertain. How would she support herself financially? Where would she live? It was these questions – and hundreds more like them – that made her decide not to tell her mum. For now.

'Have you got any plans today?' Carol asked.

Alex spread a thick layer of strawberry jam onto her toast.

'I'm going to meet Emma for lunch,' she lied, avoiding her mother's gaze, her eyes set on the knife in her hand.

'That'll be nice. It's supposed to be a warm day.'

Alex smiled and took a bite of her toast.

'Things will get better, you know that don't you?'

'I know, Mum. I'm sorry I've not been very good company lately.'

'Oh now, don't you go worrying about that. We all go through rough patches, but you're tough.'

'You think so?'

'I *know* so.' She got up and cleared away her plate. Alex got the impression that she was biting back words, stopping herself from saying things that she'd been holding in all this time. She looked at Alex and her lips parted briefly, then she turned away and refilled the kettle.

———

Alex knew the city centre would be busy on a Saturday, but the feeling of being exposed and vulnerable among crowds was overshadowed by the promise of safety in numbers. She didn't want to find herself alone with this man. She didn't want to be with him at all, it went against everything her gut told her to do, but she needed answers. Had he taken advantage of her? Or was he in the same situation as Alex – his memory of that night blurred by alcohol? Was it possible that they were both equally as drunk? Or did – as she hoped with a lurching desperation – nothing happen at all, and Ryan was in fact the father?

She'd been researching male infertility on the internet and had read countless stories about miracle conceptions and men who had, with the odds stacked against them, fathered a child. She knew what she was hoping would happen when Henry arrived – that he would tell her she was wrong and they had absolutely not had sex. She would even be okay with him making a scene, shouting and storming off in front of everyone, indignant in the face of Alex's questions. His outrage would be reassuring. This is what she clung on to.

She arrived early and sat in the same space as the day before, on the steps by the fountains, her arms encircling her knees as she became lost in the rush of the water. She'd considered – laying awake in the early hours of the morning – that she didn't need to know what had happened; that she could just have this baby and raise it on her own. But deep down, she knew that wasn't something she could do. She wanted answers. She *needed* answers.

'Alex?'

She looked away from the fountains and up at the man standing in front of her. The sun was high in the sky and she squinted at its brightness before putting her hand up to shield her eyes. Henry was wearing a pair of beige chino shorts and a black T-shirt. His trainers were bright white – they looked brand-new. He took off his sunglasses and smiled at her, tucking them into the neckline of his top.

Alex stood and smoothed down the front of her jeans. 'Hi.' Her voice sounded formal. Firm.

'Here you go.' He handed her a takeaway Starbucks cup which she took from him.

'Thank you. Shall we sit?'

'Here?' He looked around, clearly not expecting her to suggest they conduct their first date on a step in the middle of the city, while busy shoppers pushed past them and weaved their way through the crowds. Beside them, a group of young men were shouting loudly, a long plume of smoke from one of their cigarettes reaching Henry's nose.

'Yes, if that's okay?'

'Are you sure you don't want to go somewhere... with seats? There's a park not too far away or a nice bar up the road?'

'If it's okay with you, I'd just like to talk to you here for a minute first.'

'Okay, of course.'

They sat on the step, coffees in hand, Alex doing her best to keep enough distance between them so they didn't physically touch. Henry put his sunglasses back on and she felt suddenly at a disadvantage, not being able to see into his eyes. She'd always thought a person's eyes told you a lot about them; she thought of Ryan's, the brightest blue, and the way they carried his emotions so clearly.

'Have you had a good week?' he asked.

'Yes, it was okay.'

'To be honest, I'm a little surprised to hear from you. What's it been? Three months?'

'Thereabouts, yes.'

'I just assumed you weren't interested.'

'Things have been a little complicated,' she said, trying to keep her voice level. Her throat felt tight and dry. She brought the coffee to her lips and sipped at it through a small spout in the lid.

'Oh,' he said flatly. 'Are they still?'

'Actually, yes. That's what I wanted to talk to you about.' Alex turned to face him and was surprised to see he'd pushed his sunglasses up on top of his head and was staring at her intently. A strand of his wavy hair fell loose and he brushed it away.

'Okay...' There was a look on his face – something similar to amusement but not quite. She got the feeling that he was aware of her nervousness and was enjoying it. She cleared her throat.

'I recently found out that I'm pregnant.'

'Oh, wow. Okay.' He looked away from her, his elbows resting on his knees, hunched forward so she could no longer see his face. She waited for a minute, the silence hanging there between them, and eventually he turned back towards her. 'I'm sorry if this question sounds... well, very ungentlemanly... but is it mine?'

'That's the thing,' she said, trying to keep her tone neutral. 'I don't remember anything about that night. You said you'd slept on the sofa.'

'I did. But I *think* that's also where we… I think we had sex. My memory isn't so good. I remember you thrusting a bottle of vodka at me the minute we walked through the door. I've never been able to tolerate spirits.'

Alex put her head in her hands. It felt as though the last spark of hope had just been put out. 'Oh, God.' She exhaled heavily into her hands and closed her eyes. She wanted to shut out the world; to retreat into a place where the truth couldn't reach her.

'I'm sorry. We were wasted, Alex. I can barely remember anything from your place.'

'But we definitely had sex?' Her words were muffled against her hands.

'I remember us kissing, and I remember you undressing. It's more of a deduction than a certainty, but I think so.'

Alex felt her shoulders begin to shudder and her heart break even further.

'Look, Alex, I'm not going to run away from my responsibilities. I'll play as much of a role in this baby's life as you're comfortable with. I'll be there for you both, if that's what you want. Okay?'

Alex let her hands drop from her face so that she could see him. The sunlight glowed in his amber eyes, and he smiled thinly as she searched them. She didn't know what to do with the information he'd told her. They were both drunk, both single. She couldn't exactly hold it against him that her memory was more blurred than his, could she?

'I need to think about it,' she said.

'Of course. Take your time. There's no pressure from me either way, okay?'

She nodded. She realised that the conversation between them was on the better end of the enormous scale she'd concocted in her head and, although not at all what she'd been hoping for, at least Henry wasn't trying to force her into having an abortion or shirking his responsibilities. He'd told her he'd be there for her and the baby, and that was something, wasn't it? 'I think I'd better go.'

'Can we arrange to meet again, when you're ready?'

'I'll text you,' she said, getting up off the step and holding her tepid coffee in her hand.

Henry stood and pressed his lips together tightly. 'I'm sorry you're having to go through this. I want to be there for you, so please do give me a text when you're ready to talk.' There was a pleading tone to his voice and Alex realised he seemed nervous, fidgeting on his feet, his hands fiddling with the paper coffee cup.

He wasn't sure whether he would hear from her again, she could tell; all the unanswered text messages and phone calls over the past weeks had unnerved him and made him think she would drift back into silence. The way he looked at her made her feel fragile, as though he was scared a sudden movement would spook her and force her to retreat into the shadows with his child, never to be seen again. She wasn't sure whether his doubts were entirely without merit, but she answered him with all the confidence she could gather.

'I will.'

CHAPTER TWENTY-SEVEN

'Alex?'

She felt a cool hand on her shoulder, trying to rouse her from a light dream-filled sleep. She'd seen images of Ryan; they'd flitted between good and bad, comforting and distressing. She tried to open her eyes but found she couldn't, they were too heavy.

'Alex?'

She pushed against the force compelling her to drift back into the grey space between sleep and wakefulness – the place where she could try to control her dreams though often failed. It was worth it, she thought, for the fleeting moments where she could see Ryan as she remembered him, his dark hair against the white pillowcase, his eyes glistening in the sun which crept in through her window.

'Sweetheart?'

Alex pushed harder, straining to open her eyes then squinting against the light, her mum's face blurry as the sleep lingered. She rubbed at them, trying to force away the fatigue.

'There's someone here to see you.'

Suddenly, she was awake, the dark depths of sleep a distant

memory, a surge of energy rushing through her body at her mum's words. *There's someone here to see you.* Who? Ryan? She tried not to let the hope begin to rise. She sat up against the headboard and swallowed hard; her mouth was dry, her throat tight.

She felt sick. She *always* felt sick now. She couldn't work out whether it was the pregnancy or just the general state of her life. She was beginning to think it was the latter – wasn't the morning sickness supposed to end after the first trimester? By her calculations, she must be thirteen weeks along.

'Who?' she asked, her voice croaky. She cleared her throat.

The mattress dipped as her mum sat on the edge of the bed. 'A gentleman.' She smiled, her eyebrows rising as she spoke – she was excited, Alex could tell; excited at the possibility of a distraction.

Alex's flash of hope quickly vanished; her stomach turned. Her mum had met Ryan, she would remember his face after everything that had happened. It wasn't him, and it probably never would be. Why had she allowed herself, no matter how briefly, to imagine Ryan standing downstairs? What did she think was going to happen, that he'd tell her he would leave his family and raise her baby as his own?

'A gentleman?' she asked, turning round so her feet found the floor. 'Who?'

'Henry.' Her mum patted her gently on the knee. 'Nice-looking chap.'

Alex felt the colour drain from her face. 'What does he want?'

'I didn't ask. Alex, what's wrong?'

'Nothing. Nothing's wrong, Mum.' She attempted to smile but it felt more like a grimace. How had he managed to find her here, at her parents' house? Had she told him where they lived? She rubbed her temples with the tips of her fingers, trying to remember, but the truth was she had no idea. She couldn't recall what they'd talked about that night. She could have given him her national insurance number and bank details for all she knew.

Her mum took her hand and held it on her lap. 'Do you want me to tell him you're not feeling well?'

Alex thought for a moment. It had been a week since they'd met in Nottingham and he'd tried to contact her several times since. It had annoyed her, the fact that he'd reached out before she'd felt ready. She knew she had to face him sooner or later, to try to build some kind of rapport with this man with whom she had created a life, but at the same time she couldn't help feeling as though she wanted to crawl back into bed and hide from it all.

'No, it's okay, I'll be down in a minute.'

Her mum smiled weakly and got up from the bed, walking over to the window and opening the curtains fully. Light flooded in, carrying the warmth of the summer with it.

'You take your time, I'll make some tea.'

———

Alex washed her face and brushed her teeth before rummaging around the piles of clothes on her bedroom floor, looking for something clean. She found a pair of denim shorts and a white T-shirt at the end of her bed and put them on.

She could hear the low hum of conversation downstairs, her mum's soft honeyed tone interspersed with something less familiar – the deep voice of a man. It sounded out of place and it struck Alex how infrequently she heard her dad moving around the house, his deep, raspy voice reserved for the odd occasion where he would respond briefly to something her mum had said.

Alex kept her footing light on the stairs, careful not to make a sound, and she realised she was hoping to eavesdrop, to catch a slice of the conversation which had been ticking along while she'd been upstairs. She was curious. What was Henry telling her mum? She suddenly felt her heartrate quicken – would he assume her mum knew about the pregnancy? Near the bottom step she could just make out their words.

'...always wanted to live in a little village like this myself, actually. I'm getting tired of the city life.'

'It's a beautiful place. Very quiet,' came her mum's voice. 'The woodland was Alex's favourite place when she was little, she loved exploring.'

'I can imagine. It's the perfect playground for a child. Kids these days are all screens and electronics; it's not good for them.'

'No, there was none of that in my day. We didn't even have a landline until Alex was a teenager. Of course, more for her benefit than ours.'

Alex took the last couple of steps then walked down the hallway and turned into the kitchen. Henry was sat on one side of the table and her mum on the other, each with a cup of tea in front of them. A plate of cherry scones sat in the middle, the butter dish open to the side. Henry beamed at her as she entered the room. He pushed his glasses up the bridge of his nose with his forefinger then stood, the chair legs scraping against the kitchen floor as he moved towards her.

'Alex! Good to see you.' He moved closer to her and, after a moment of brief hesitation, he bent down and kissed her on the cheek. Alex's eyes darted to her mum who sat watching them, smiling. 'How are you? You look well.'

She brushed her fingers through her unwashed hair and felt the tangle of lugs which had accumulated. She suddenly felt self-conscious. Henry was immaculately groomed, dressed in a pair of jeans and a blue short-sleeved shirt. Her mum stood and began to clear away the empty cups from the table. Henry didn't turn round, he continued to watch Alex, trying to catch her eye.

'I'll make you a cup of tea then I'll get out of the way.' Her mum began busying herself at the kitchen worktop. 'Henry, would you like another?'

He turned to face her. 'If it's not too much trouble.'

'Not at all.'

Alex watched as her mum set the cups on the saucers and placed a teaspoon on the side. She'd taken out the good china, the ones reserved especially for guests. Henry had turned back to face her and Alex could tell from the intensity in his eyes that he was desperate to be alone with her.

'How are you?' he asked.

She looked nervously between Henry and her mum who had her back to them, trying to convey that she hadn't yet told her about the baby. 'I'm okay, thank you. Shall we sit?'

'Here, let me.' He pulled out a chair for her, next to where he'd been sitting, and Alex had to bite the inside of her cheek to stop herself from telling him she was capable of picking her own seat in the kitchen she'd known her whole life. She knew he was just trying to be chivalrous – or perhaps he actually *was* chivalrous – but it felt forced and unnatural. A deliberate act meant to impress.

'Have you had a good week?' he asked, taking the seat next to her.

'It was okay.'

Her mum placed two cups of tea down on the table. The spoons clinked against the china. 'I'm going to go out to the garden. Help yourself to a scone, won't you?'

'Thank you, Mrs Vaughn, it's been lovely meeting you.'

'Please, call me Carol.'

'If you insist!' Henry beamed and pulled his tea towards him.

Alex watched as her mum gave her an encouraging smile before she left. She knew she wanted her to make an effort, to try to look past the fact that this wasn't Ryan; to see the man who sat before her, untainted by the impression another man had left. She wanted her to break out of this prison she'd created for herself, but Alex wasn't sure it was that simple. She looked over her shoulder as her mum closed the door, then Alex turned back to Henry.

'Alex, I know I said to take your time but when you didn't respond to my messages or answer my calls…'

'It's only been a week!'

'Yes, but…'

'But what?' She suddenly felt angry at him for turning up, uninvited, in the only space that felt remotely unspoiled to her now. 'Am I not making a decision quick enough for you? This life-changing decision that will affect me significantly more than it will affect *you*?'

Henry took a deep breath, his amber eyes flicking down to the table before returning to her. 'No, that's not it. I'm sorry if it seems like I'm pressuring you, that's not my intention at all. I was rather hoping we could talk, or that you might want me to be involved in the decision-making or… or… I don't know, Alex, I was going crazy sitting around waiting to find out whether I'm going to be a dad.'

When he finished talking Alex noticed his eyes were glistening with tears. She suddenly lost the spark of anger that had forced itself to the forefront of her mind a moment earlier. She realised that there was a part of her that was deliberately dragging it out, refusing to tell him that she'd already made up her mind. She was keeping the baby. Why was she so reluctant to tell him? It had felt like her decision and hers alone, but hearing his words – hearing him refer to himself as the *dad* – it stirred something in her. She felt sorry for him, she realised. This baby was as much his at it was hers.

'No, *I'm* sorry.' She let out a long sigh. 'I'm sorry I haven't been in touch, it's just… it's…'

He placed a hand over hers on the table. 'It's okay. You don't need to explain.'

'I'm keeping the baby.' The words came out hurried and she didn't look at him as she spoke, but she felt his hand squeeze hers and heard the unmistakeable sigh of relief. When she looked up, the tears that had welled in his eyes fell freely.

'I was hoping you'd say that.'

'Really?'

'More than anything.'

They sat like that for a while, their tea going cold in front of them and their fingers entwined on the table. All the things they were yet to discuss occupied every available space around them; Alex felt the weight of it all but refused to give in – she wanted a moment to experience the joy of a pregnancy she had not yet allowed herself to feel happy about.

Everything else could wait.

CHAPTER TWENTY-EIGHT

They sat in the garden enjoying the midday sunshine, a blanket on the grass and Alex's mum back inside. Henry had suggested they take a walk to 'talk things over,' but Alex couldn't face parading around Elwood with Henry, partly because she was afraid she'd bump into Ryan and partly because she was afraid she would bump into just about anyone who knew what had happened.

She hadn't told Henry about the incident with Mia or the fact she'd left her job before she was pushed, and she hadn't told him about Ryan. She knew it would come up sooner or later but she was hoping for the latter, after the initial awkwardness between them had dissipated and things felt slightly less raw.

'Have you let work know yet?' he asked. 'That you're pregnant?'

Alex felt her stomach drop. She should have known her job would come up in conversation early on, but she'd allowed herself to hope that she might at least get the day.

'No, I...' she stammered, caught between truth and lies and half-truths. 'I don't actually work at the school anymore.'

'Oh?' His brow furrowed.

'I handed in my notice not long after the Easter holidays.'

'Oh,' he said again, as though drawing his own conclusions. 'Because of the pregnancy?'

'No... I... I...' She was searching for words that seemed to evade her.

'People have one-night stands or flings, Alex. It's nothing to be ashamed of.' He took her hand and held it gently in his. 'I'm sorry you felt you had to leave your job.' He looked genuinely upset. Alex knew she should correct him, but the words she was formulating in her mind never made it out of her mouth. He squeezed her hand. 'I can help out financially, I have some savings and–'

'No, that won't be necessary. I've sold my apartment and I'm going to look for another job.'

'While you're pregnant? But you won't get maternity pay, will you?'

'No, I don't suppose I will, but I could use my savings to cover the time I'll have off then go back once the baby is old enough.'

'How long are you planning to have off?'

'I don't know, I hadn't really thought about it.' Alex felt under pressure all of a sudden, as though she were fending off questions aimed at highlighting how naïve she'd been. 'I guess a few months.'

Henry's mouth tightened and she couldn't work out what emotion he was trying to suppress; annoyance? Amusement? Concern?

'Alex, I'll support you with whatever you decide, okay? But so you have all the options on the table...' He readjusted himself so he was sat up a little straighter, looking directly at her. 'My place has two bedrooms and it's not too far from here. I'm not suggesting we move in together in a romantic way, but you are more than welcome to the spare room. That way, I could help you with the baby, do some of the night feeds and nappy changes, and you wouldn't have to worry about money.'

Alex didn't respond at first, she needed to take a minute to process what Henry was suggesting. She jumped chaotically from thinking it was a nice gesture to feeling overwhelmed and even a little angry at how presumptuous he was being. Yes, they were having a baby together, but how had he managed to equate that to her wanting to *live* with him?

'Henry, I don't think we know each other well enough to live together.'

'No, maybe not at the moment, but I wanted you to know it's an option down the line. If we spend some time together and you think it's something you might want, then let me know. No pressure.'

'Okay.' She didn't know whether she should thank him or whether he would misconstrue that as something more than she intended. The truth was, she didn't know this man. She didn't know what made him tick. She didn't know what made him happy or angry or sad. It seemed as though it was going to require a lot of effort on her part to try to learn all of those things. To understand him. But she had to, because they were tied together, by something that at the moment was no bigger than a peach but, soon, would be their whole life. They would be a family – irregular and unconventional, maybe, but a family nonetheless. And Henry *wanted* to be involved.

She watched as he picked at the grass absent-mindedly, lost in thought, and she made a decision; she decided that she would at least try, in whatever way she felt able to, to make the best of the situation she'd found herself in, because he was there. He'd showed up. And that was more than Alex had ever had from her own dad.

'Have you scheduled an appointment with a midwife? Or your GP?'

Alex glanced nervously towards the house but her mum was nowhere to be seen. 'No, I will, I just need to tell my parents first.'

'How come you haven't told them yet?'

'It hasn't felt like the right time. It's not exactly how I hoped I'd be telling them they were going to be grandparents.' She realised she was referring to her parents as a unified front – a couple – but what she really meant was her mum. Alex always imagined she would be in a relationship when she found out she was pregnant. That she would be able to tell her mum she was going to be a grandma and her automatically know who the father was. Alex realised she felt ashamed, and more than a little guilty. Her mum had had enough to deal with lately, and now she was about to pile this on top of her as well. The only silver lining was that Carol had met Henry, and she seemed to like him.

'Your mum seems nice, I can't imagine her being angry.'

'No, she won't be. But she'll worry. It's not every mother's dream to see their child pregnant after a one-night stand. Especially one they don't even remember.' Alex regretted saying the last part as soon as the words left her mouth. Henry seemed to physically withdraw, a look of embarrassment in his eyes.

'Well,' he said, clearing his throat. 'I was rather hoping we could leave the details out.'

'Lie, you mean?'

He shrugged. 'Sugar coat the truth, maybe? All I mean is, she doesn't have to know everything. You could tell her we went out on a few dates.'

Alex weighed it up for a moment in her mind. Maybe he was right. She could soften the blow, add in a few dates. 'I'll think about it.' She stifled a yawn, tiredness suddenly consuming her. The emotions of the day had added to the existing fatigue.

'Tired?'

'All the time.'

'I read that most women begin to feel better during the second trimester.'

'You've been reading about pregnant women?'

'Yes, a little.' He looked coy, as though he'd revealed a secret about himself that he hadn't wanted to share. 'I wanted to know what you were going through. Did you have any morning sickness?'

'I felt sick *all* the time. I still do, really, but it's been more difficult lately to decide whether that's the baby or the stress.'

Henry's eyes were full of concern; Alex noticed them flit from her face to her belly and back again. She wondered whether the concern was for her and what she was dealing with, or whether it was purely for the baby. Maybe, she reasoned, it was a little of both.

'If there's anything I can do to help make things less stressful for you... even if it's just bringing you the food you're craving in the middle of the night. Seriously, I'll keep my phone on loud, you can call me anytime.'

Alex almost laughed. Almost. She yawned again but this time she didn't try to hide it. 'I think I just need to sleep.'

Henry nodded and got to his feet then held his hand out to Alex. She took it and he pulled her up. When she was standing she realised how close they were all of a sudden, her nose almost touching his chest. She looked up at him and saw flecks of brown in his amber eyes; they seemed to shimmer in the sunlight.

He brushed his fingers through his hair and smiled. 'I'll let you get some rest. Think about what I said, and let me know if you need anything, okay?'

'Okay.'

She walked with him to the house and opened the gate that led down to a little entry at the side, out to the front of the property; that way they wouldn't have to see her mum again, to go through the monotony of small talk before he left. Alex had been alone so frequently lately that it had taken so much out of her to be with someone else, to have to fake that she was okay – a functioning human who got up in a morning and drank tea and ate scones. She was emotionally and physically drained.

'Where's your car?' she asked, noticing the absence of another vehicle on the drive.

'I parked in Elwood and walked.'

'Actually, I meant to ask, how did you know where to find me?'

'You told me.' When Alex looked at him, confused, he added, 'The night we met in Nottingham, you told me about where you grew up. You said it was the old farmhouse next to the woodland in Elwood.'

'But how did you know I'd be here?'

'I went to your apartment and someone else was living there, so that was my first clue.'

'Oh.'

'Yes. So this was my last shot. I'm sorry if it was a bit much, me being here, but I was going crazy.'

Alex nodded. 'I understand.'

'Speak soon?' he asked, shoving his hands into his pockets and shuffling on his feet.

'Yes, I'll be in touch.'

He turned and walked over the cobbled driveway, skimming the trees which led out onto Beck Lane. She stood and watched, her mind trying to recall telling him about where she grew up, but try as she might, she could not conjure the memory.

CHAPTER TWENTY-NINE

Alex had been trying to work up the courage to tell her mum about the baby ever since Henry had left. It had been four days and the courage still had not materialised. She hadn't been out of the house since Henry's visit and it was as though the walls were closing in on her, trapping her and her thoughts. She needed to think. She needed to let her mind wander and land upon the best way to break it to her mum. Alex needed to run.

She dressed in a pair of shorts and a loose-fitting vest – she hadn't started to show yet but loose clothing had come to feel like an additional form of defence, a barrier that made her secret safer. Carol was in the garden when she went outside, hunched over a spot of wildflowers at the front of the house. She looked up when she heard Alex open the door.

'Off for a run?'

'Just a short one around the woodland.'

Carol smiled. 'Good. I think you'll feel better for it.'

'I hope so.'

Alex stretched against the wall of the house, the ivy cool beneath her hands as she watched her mum picking out the weeds that had infiltrated the flowers. She had to quash the overwhelming urge to tell her everything.

'See you later, Mum.'

'Enjoy your run.'

Alex walked the length of the driveway then turned towards the entrance to the woods, listening for anything other than her own footsteps. An uneasy feeling had crept into her chest; she put it down to her trepidation about seeing Ryan or Hannah or someone else from school, but she wasn't entirely sure that was true. She still hadn't completely shaken off the feeling of being watched, the one that had consumed her in the days leading up to Mia's accident. She stood under the shade of an old oak, her eyes scanning between the trees. After a couple of minutes of waiting, hearing nothing but the gentle sound of the wind and the birds, she started her watch and set off at a jog.

She took the main path then forked off to the right, towards the edge of the forest and away from the stream. She kicked onwards, her breathing steady, careful not to exert herself too much: she was thinking about the baby. She still hadn't booked an appointment with a midwife – she knew she was delaying the inevitability of having to move surgeries to the local one where the receptionists lived around the corner and knew everyone who walked through its doors. She didn't want everyone knowing her business; the thought of sitting in the waiting room with a handful of locals and being called in by the midwife filled her with dread. Everyone would assume it was Ryan's baby and, in Elwood, gossip spread like fire.

The path led back through the woodland and met with the grassy area – the secret garden which felt tainted by tragedy. Alex stopped, her hands clutching the splintered wood of the picnic table – the one that Ryan had once sat at with Hannah as their eyes met nervously, on the cusp of something neither could have predicted. She waited for her breathing to calm, her back hunched and her eyes filling with tears she hadn't realised were forming.

When it had ended with Ryan she'd told herself that things would get better – that the ache in her chest would begin to ease and her heart would heal. Time, that was all she needed, and the pain would start to go away. As she tried to remember that now, she struggled to recall whether she knew she was lying even back then. Fooling herself with words meant for simpler things.

Blinking tears away, she inhaled slowly, perched on the edge of the table to give herself a minute to regroup. To think. But as she did, she heard something – the sound of twigs snapping underfoot followed by a couple of heavy footsteps. Her eyes darted around, trying to locate where it was coming from, hardly daring to breathe. *Crack.* She heard it again, the unmistakeable sound of twigs breaking, followed by a flurry of movement in the undergrowth.

She stepped away from it, backwards towards an opening between two trees, then onto the path which skirted the woodland. She began to run, away from whatever or whoever had invaded her moment of peace, along the path which led back to the entrance. Just before she got there, she saw something in the distance – a flash of colour between the tree trunks. She stopped running and waited, her breathing laboured and her heart racing. A noise echoed between the trees, low and indistinct. A voice.

She looked over her shoulder, wondering whether to run the other way, towards the back of the woods that led onto the fields. She could get onto the road there, eventually. Before she'd made up her mind, the flash of colour moved out onto the path, and with a jolt to her stomach she realised it was Hannah. She was holding something up to her cheek and it took Alex a moment to realise it was a mobile phone. Hannah looked at her, frozen, then she lowered her arm, the phone still clutched in her hand.

Alex didn't know what to say or do, or whether to do anything at all. Her whole body was trembling, her lips parted as though about to speak, but the words never came. Hannah was staring right at her, her eyes full of hatred. Alex had an overwhelming urge to run away, but before she could move, Hannah had spun round and was disappearing between the trees and out onto Beck Lane. Alex stood listening to the distant sounds of Hannah's footsteps, wondering how long she'd been there. And why.

————

The days ticked by without change. Another weekend passed and slipped seamlessly into another week. The summer had been long and dry and the intensity of it only seemed to echo her own turmoil; the relentless discomfort. It was suffocating. Alex still felt weighed down by the secret she was keeping, her throat tightening every time she was alone with her mum, her body restricting the words that were desperate to be unleashed.

Henry had tried calling her several times, and when she hadn't answered he'd sent her messages asking how she was and whether she'd booked an appointment with the midwife yet. She'd replied saying she was tired and that she'd be in touch soon, hoping that would placate him. Every time she saw his name flash up on her phone, she felt the knot in her stomach tighten. She still hadn't managed to make sense of what had happened, nor had she managed to forget Ryan. To stop loving him. She needed time. Perhaps more than she had.

She knew she wasn't being particularly fair to Henry – he'd been kind and reasonable and all of the things he hadn't necessarily needed to be, but it always came back to the same simple yet gut-wrenching truth: he wasn't Ryan, and her heart ached because of it.

On Friday morning she woke with an urge that felt too big to contain. She paced her bedroom then made a cup of tea that she didn't drink, then she sat out in the garden trying to read a book. Her eyes scanned the words but her brain couldn't make sense of them. It refused to engage; refused to be distracted.

Midday came and went but the urge did not leave. She needed to see Ryan, or at least speak to him. Perhaps what she needed, she reasoned, was closure. A conversation. An end to this chapter of her life so that she could start the next. She reached for her phone and checked the time – almost two. He'd still be at work. She typed out a message.

> I know this is out of the blue, but could we meet? I just want to talk.

She pressed send then held her phone in her hand, watching for the little dots that told her he was typing. She waited for what seemed like an eternity but, in reality, was little more than ten minutes. When she saw that he was replying her breath caught in her throat. What if he said no? She clutched the phone with both hands as she sat out in the garden, her legs stretched out on a blanket among the grass. When his response came she exhaled slowly, releasing the breath she'd been holding.

> Okay, but not round here. Can you remember where we parked when we went to Win Hill?

Alex wondered how it was possible that reading a simple text could have such an impact on her. She felt her shoulders relax and her breathing calm. She felt weightless. She told herself not to get carried away. It didn't mean anything. They weren't running away together; there would be no happily ever after. But the words sank as quickly as they came and the intention behind them evaporated. It was a tiny ray of hope, but one she clutched on to with everything she had. She pressed reply.

I remember. When?

A minute later, he'd responded.

I can be there for six?

Alex held the phone to her chest and closed her eyes. It felt like a momentary reprieve, but one she gladly welcomed.

CHAPTER THIRTY

Alex didn't remember the way; she could recall the car park but not the route to it, so she found the postcode online and typed it into the Google Maps app which told her it would take her just over an hour to get there.

She left at 4.30 on account of the potential traffic and was relieved to have had the extra time – there were roadworks just outside Bakewell that added almost half an hour onto her journey and by the time she turned up it was almost quarter past six.

She saw Ryan's car as soon as she turned into the car park; he'd pulled into a bay in the furthest corner where a large ash tree blocked the sun which had begun its slow descent towards the horizon. A flock of magpies sat perched on a rickety wooden fence and as Alex pulled into the bay beside Ryan she counted them absent-mindedly, a throwback from childhood when her mum would recite the familiar rhyme to her.

There were six as she pulled in but, at the last second, another joined them. *Seven*, she thought, recalling her mum's sing-song voice.

"One for sorrow, two for joy, three for a girl, four for a boy, five for silver, six for gold, seven for a secret never to be told."

She switched the engine off and unbuckled her seat belt. Ryan's eyes were already on her when she turned and it took her the briefest of moments to recognise him. He looked different, but she couldn't put her finger on why. He got out of his car and Alex followed his lead, stepping out and walking to meet him somewhere in the middle.

'Hey.' His voice was quiet but it seemed to carry so much – the uncertainty and the pain Alex understood so well – and in that moment she realised that he'd been feeling all of the things she'd been feeling, the heartbreak and the hopelessness. Those things weren't reserved just for her.

'Hey.'

'Do you want to walk or...' He let his sentence hang there, waiting for her to take the lead. The car park was quiet, just another couple of vehicles at the other side and a lone motorbike parked in the middle. She didn't feel like walking, she felt like sitting with him somewhere so not a single word could be lost among the vastness of the land. She wanted to contain their conversation and themselves within the confines of something solid.

'Actually, I think I would rather we just sat?'

'Sure.' He glanced over his shoulder to his car before turning back to face her. 'Hop in.'

She did as he said, opening the passenger door and climbing inside, refusing to acknowledge Mia's car seat in the back or the various different things that spoke of his family. She noticed him quickly stuffing something into the compartment in his door and she knew without having to see it that it was something belonging to Hannah.

Alex shut the door. 'Thanks for meeting me.'

He nodded. 'How have you been?'

Her instinct was to lie, to tell him she'd been okay, but she realised that was not why she was there. It might be her last chance to tell him everything – she didn't want to hold anything back. 'Not very good, actually. You?'

'About the same.' He'd angled his body towards her but his eyes seemed restless, unable to settle on her without flicking back and forth to the window. He looked forlorn; a man who wore his pain for all to see. He'd lost weight and his eyes seemed to have dulled, the blueness dialled back to grey.

'It's been the hardest few months of my life.'

He looked at her, his eyes suddenly still. 'Mine too.' He reached out and took her hand in his and her heart raced at the feel of his skin against hers. She wanted more. She wanted to crawl onto his lap and kiss him; she wanted to rest her cheek in the curve of his neck and breathe him in; she wanted to hold him in her arms and never let go.

'I miss you. I miss you more than I ever thought it was possible to miss someone and I don't know what to do anymore. I don't know what to do!' She was crying. She felt that all she did was cry, and when she wasn't crying she was holding back the tears that were always lingering. It was exhausting.

Ryan reached his other hand across and held it against her cheek, wiping away her tears with his thumb. 'Hey,' he whispered. 'Don't cry.'

'I can't lie anymore, Ryan. I can't lie to myself or to you or to anyone else. I love you. I want to be with you.'

His head dropped and his hand moved down to her knee. She wondered if she'd said too much, pushed too hard, but she hadn't come there to bite back words. She'd spent too long doing that. When he looked back up she saw that his eyes were damp with his own tears.

'I...' he began, but his voice caught in his throat and he inhaled sharply before trying again. 'I love you too.' She waited for the *but*, dreading its inevitable arrival. The silence dragged out, their hands entwined, and she wondered whether he was

N. A. COOPER

allowing time to pass before he continued so he didn't taint those three words with whatever else was to come. 'I don't have the answers, Alex, I'm sorry. I don't know how to fix this. I don't... I don't think it's fixable.'

It wasn't the *but* she'd been dreading – he'd managed to disguise it as something else – but she knew what it meant. Nothing had changed.

'Because of Mia?' Alex asked, though she already knew the answer.

'Because of Mia. Because I'm her dad, and she needs me around.'

As painful as it was and as much as it wasn't what she'd wanted to hear, it made Alex love him all the more for his dedication to her.

'What are you going to do about the baby?' he asked.

Alex rested her head back and looked out of the window, at the shadows cast by the sun filtering through the ash tree. 'I'm going to have the baby,' she said. 'As for everything else... I have no idea.'

He squeezed her hand. 'You're stronger than you think, Alex. You can do this, I know you can.'

'But I don't want to do this alone. I wish...' She paused, not knowing if she should say any more.

'What do you wish?'

She turned back to face him, looking him directly in the eye. 'I wish this baby was yours, and that none of this was complicated. I wish we could be together without anybody getting hurt.'

He looked away, his eyes set somewhere in the distance. Alex watched him before he turned back to face her.

'I wish that were possible.'

Alex didn't know which part he was referring to, and she didn't ask.

She wanted to talk to him about Hannah, to see whether he thought she was capable of seeking revenge. She thought back to the scratch across the side of her car; the knock on her door while Ryan was there; the car that seemed to follow him when he left; the word SLUT on her windscreen. It all seemed to make sense except the flowers: why would Hannah send her flowers?

'I saw Hannah earlier in the week.'

'Yeah, she mentioned that.'

This surprised Alex but she wasn't immediately sure why. In her head, she didn't think they had the kind of relationship where Hannah would tell him such things; Alex liked to think of them as leading almost entirely separate lives. She realised that she'd made that conclusion to fit with her own narrative, to make it easier to excuse their affair. 'I wasn't sure whether she'd tell you. She ran off.'

'I don't think she expected to see you. Mr Pratchett had lost his dog – there were a few people out looking for him on Wednesday. That's why she was in the woods.'

Alex took a moment, unsure whether to ask anything further. 'I wasn't sure if she was there looking for...' She swallowed, the words sounding odd now they'd been spoken.

'For what?'

'Well... me.'

Ryan frowned. 'No, I think she wants as much distance between you as possible.'

'It's just... how she acted at the school... she *hates* me.'

Ryan shook his head. 'No, she doesn't hate you, Alex. She hates what we did. She hates that I lied to her.'

'How are things... between you?' Alex bit her lip, bracing herself for his response.

'They're probably as you'd expect, considering.' He took a deep breath as though preparing himself to ask the next question. 'The guy...' he began, his tone uncertain. 'Is he going to be involved?'

Alex didn't want to talk about Henry. She knew he was a big part of her life but she couldn't help but think of him as an irrelevance. She hoped that, one day, that might change, and she might be able to see all the good in him rather than things she felt he'd taken away. If they hadn't slept together, would she and Ryan still stand a chance? Could they have rekindled their affair, a secret romance they hid until Mia was older?

Alex pinched the bridge of her nose and closed her eyes tight. She couldn't think about that. 'I think so. He wants to be but...'

'But what?'

'He's not you.'

'You can't hold that against him, Alex.'

'Can't I?'

'I want you to be happy. I want you to have the future you deserve. You will love this baby more than you could *ever* love me – I promise you that.'

A sob escaped her mouth and she quickly covered it with her hand, attempting to mask the rest which followed. She could feel it – this was the end she knew would come, the closure she needed but desperately wanted to delay. It felt cruel. Intolerable.

Ryan leaned across and held her as she cried into his shoulder, her hands against his back, her fingertips digging into his skin in desperation. Maybe if she held him hard enough he would feel how much she needed him. Maybe if she refused to let go he would never leave her.

But he did, just as she always feared he would.

She stayed behind for a while after he'd gone, watching the land and the birds. One by one the magpies left her until only one remained, perched on the wall, its beady black eyes watching her inquisitively.

One for sorrow.

She turned on her engine and reversed out of the bay, turning the car around until she was facing the road. She was wrong, she knew that now: seeing him *had* made her feel worse, it had shattered her already fragile heart again.

The light was beginning to fade, the sun hiding among the

hills to the west. The remainder of its light seeped into the cloudless sky, hanging on, refusing to let go. She looked in her rear-view mirror and saw the streaks of blood-red glowing behind her. The magpie took off, soaring into the sky, leaving an empty space behind.

She edged out of the car park, the tyres crunching against gravel, and arched her neck forward to see around a tight bend. To the right, a hundred metres or so further down the road, a grey hatchback was pulled over in a lay-by, partially obscured by an overgrown hedgerow.

Alex squinted, her eyes narrowing as she tried to make out the shadowy silhouette of a figure inside, then straining to try to see the number plate. But before she could make any sense of it the engine sprung to life and the tyres screeched against the road. It turned, leaving nothing but a plume of dust behind.

CHAPTER THIRTY-ONE

A lex checked the rear-view mirror all the way home, looking for the grey hatchback she knew she'd seen on more than one occasion. She tried to access the memories but they were blurry, weighed down by fatigue and emotion. She'd seen it at her apartment – twice – then while she was out running. She could recall puddles on the ground – it was the day of the school trip. Then she'd seen it when she'd met Ryan by the woodland, the night she'd told him about the baby. Was she reading too much into it? Was it even the same car?

She tried to put it out of her mind, telling herself she was just being paranoid. She'd been in a constant state of stress for the past few months and it had taken its toll. She arrived back at her parents' house feeling exhausted, her eyes sore and puffy. As she turned off the engine she heard her phone vibrating from her bag on the passenger seat. She took it out and looked at the display – Henry. She knew she should answer.

She'd tried over the course of the week to put herself in his position and she realised how hard it must be, to be waiting on a call from a woman he doesn't know; a woman who's carrying his child. She realised she didn't even know whether this was his first child, or whether he had others. Had he been married before? Perhaps she should have asked, but she'd had little interest in getting to know him.

Her heart and her mind were with Ryan, and it wasn't doing her any good. The phone stopped ringing and a minute later a message popped up on the screen. She was still sitting in the car, the door open slightly and a warm summer breeze filtering in.

> Just wondered if you had any plans this weekend? Would be nice to see you.

Alex let out a groan. She couldn't keep putting off getting to know him. She had to make an effort, if not for her sake then for the sake of her baby. She typed out a response.

> No plans. Could meet for lunch tomorrow?

She watched him typing out a response until it flashed up on the screen.

> Sounds great! Meet you in Nottingham, same place as last time? 12?

She replied telling him she would see him there then dropped her phone into her bag. A light had come on in the kitchen and she could just make out her mum pottering around, opening cupboards and no doubt boiling the kettle. Alex had to fight the urge to wait outside until she'd gone to bed.

She'd never avoided her mum before, they'd always had the kind of relationship where she'd been able to tell her anything, the absence of the only man in both of their lives bonding them, the two of them against the world. Alex missed that, and she hoped that soon she would feel that closeness return, but for now she was keeping her at arm's length, concealing something that felt too big to hide.

When she knew Henry a little better, she would tell her mum

everything. She needed to feel prepared, and for that she needed information. She needed to get to know Henry, and to begin to let go of Ryan.

———

Saturday brought a reprieve from the heat that had dominated the summer so far. There were storms and flash floods predicted from late afternoon. When Alex saw the forecast she was thankful to have an excuse to get back early, in case Henry suggested spending the day together. She would have lunch with him, discuss the logistics of the pregnancy and get to know him a little better. She was still trying to work out whether she would allow him to get to know her in turn.

She'd put on a loose-fitting blue dress and grabbed her denim jacket and an umbrella, just in case the rain arrived early. As she was about to leave she'd received a text from Henry telling her he'd made reservations at a pub in the city centre. She hadn't replied, she didn't really mind where they ate, it was a struggle for her to fancy anything at all; the difficulty was distinguishing whether that was just normal pregnancy symptoms or the side effect of a broken heart.

He was waiting for her when she arrived, dressed in a pair of jeans and a navy sports jacket. She could tell he'd made an effort and she wondered if it was for her or himself; maybe he was one of those people inclined to always make the best of themselves. She knew that if she could rewind to a time before she met Ryan, she would feel excited at the prospect of a date with the man who stood in front of her, smiling, well dressed and evidently pleased to see her.

'Hi, how are you?'

She noticed his eyes slip briefly to her stomach.

'I'm okay. How are you?' They stood facing each other,

exchanging pleasantries as though they were strangers which, Alex thought, they were not far from.

'I'm good, better now you're here.' His honesty was disarming; she could remember thinking that about him the night they had met in The Garden Room. There was no pretence, no armour. Just Henry, telling her that he was pleased to see her. 'I made reservations at The Plough, did you get my text?' Alex nodded. 'Is that okay?'

'Yes, that's fine. My appetite isn't great at the moment though.'

'Are you still feeling sick?'

'Yeah, sometimes, but even when I don't I still don't feel hungry.'

'Like you said before though, that could be the stress.' Alex was surprised he'd remembered her saying that. *She* could barely remember saying that. 'How have you been otherwise?'

'Okay, just tired.'

He smiled sympathetically. 'Hopefully you'll begin to feel much better soon. What are we now, fifteen weeks along?'

It irked her that he used the word *we*. It was her carrying this baby, feeling like shit, doing the hard part. She swallowed down the annoyance but it left a bad taste in her mouth. 'Yeah, thereabouts.'

'Shall we…' He gestured towards one of the streets heading out of the square and she walked beside him. 'I don't want to sound pushy, but have you booked an appointment yet? You could be low in iron or something; that could be contributing to how tired you're feeling.'

'Look, Henry, I'll be perfectly honest with you. I have to move surgeries, and once I've moved to the local one in Elwood where everyone knows everyone's business, the word will soon get back to my parents, and I would prefer that news to come from *me*.'

'So…' He paused and Alex could tell he was trying to tread carefully. 'Why don't you tell them? I mean, what are you waiting for? I could be there when you do, if that helps?'

'No, no, that's not it. I suppose I'm just waiting until I know you better. At first I didn't *want* to tell them, but once I began thinking about *how* I would tell them, I realised my mum would ask a lot of questions. Mainly about you. And I wouldn't be able to answer them.'

'So you want to get to know me better first?'

'Yes.'

'Okay, I can understand that. So let's get to know each other.' He turned and smiled as they walked, his amber eyes darker in the grey light of the day. 'No questions are off limits, ask me anything you want.'

'Have you got any children already?'

'Nope.'

'Have you been married before?'

'No.'

'Engaged?'

'No.'

'Lived with anyone?'

'Yes, three years ago, she moved back home to America and I didn't want to go with her. We were together for...' he thought about it for a moment, 'two years, I think; lived together for one.'

'How old are you?'

'Thirty-seven.'

'Are your parents together?'

'Yes, they moved to the coast when they retired. Bridlington. I visit them every few months or so. Nice place.'

'Any siblings?'

'Only child.'

Alex paused, trying to think what else she wanted to ask. Henry waited patiently, unbothered by her sudden barrage of questions.

'Have you done anything like this before?'

He looked at her, confused. 'Like what?'

'Slept with someone and not been able to remember.'

He blushed slightly at her question and turned away, his hands slipping into the pockets of his jeans. 'No. That was a first for me and something I hope never to repeat.' Alex wondered whether she should feel insulted by his obvious pang of shame. 'That's not to say I regret it,' he continued, sensing Alex's uncertainty. 'Well, I do. But only because of the circumstances. I wish I could have taken you out and got to know you. Done things properly, you know?'

They arrived at the pub and Henry pulled open the door, standing aside to let Alex pass through. A woman greeted them both with a smile, a silver badge pinned to a crisp white shirt. *Fran.*

'I made a reservation,' Henry said. 'Henry Maguire.'

Alex made a mental note of his surname, realising that up until then she'd had no idea what it was. Would her child take his name? She hadn't really thought about it, but it was a possibility. Perhaps they would hyphenate their names. *Vaughn-Maguire* or *Maguire-Vaughn.*

The waitress led them to a booth table at the end of a large rectangular room with wooden floorboards and emerald green walls. Henry waited for Alex to slip into one side of the booth before he took the other. The waitress handed them both a menu and took their drinks order before leaving them alone. Alex's eyes scanned the menu, her stomach empty but full of nerves. Images of Ryan kept trying to push themselves into her mind and she had to summon all of her strength to drive them away.

'See anything you fancy?' Henry asked.

'Hmmm, not really. But I guess I need to eat.'

Henry closed his menu and put it to one side just as the waitress returned with their drinks. She asked if they were ready to order and Alex closed her menu, swallowing down the pang of nausea.

'I'll have the chicken wrap, please.'

Fran turned to Henry.

'Lasagne for me, please. But could you make sure the chef knows I have a nut allergy?'

'Certainly, I'll let her know. Thank you.' Fran took their menus, leaving them alone, facing each other across the table, the endless questions lurking all around them. Alex didn't know where to start.

'So, you're allergic to nuts? I feel like I know you better already.'

Henry smiled and placed his hands on the table, clasping them together.

'Yes, I have to carry an epi pen. What about you, any allergies or medical conditions?'

Alex couldn't help but laugh. If this were a normal date, questions like this would seem bizarre, but considering how their DNA was now combined, she understood.

'No, none.'

Henry smiled and looked down at the table for a moment. 'Can I ask you something else?' Alex nodded. 'You mentioned how things were complicated before, and one of the few things I remember about the night we spent together was how you told me about Ryan. I know it's none of my business who you go out with, but now that we're having a baby together... well, I guess I just wondered whether you're seeing anyone?'

'No.' Alex answered quickly, perhaps a little too quickly, and Henry seemed to physically retreat at the sharpness of her words. 'No,' she repeated, more calmly. 'That's really the last thing on my mind at the moment.'

'Okay,' he said simply.

He took a deep breath and pushed his glasses up the bridge of his nose with his forefinger. She wondered if he was waiting for her to elaborate – maybe she should, she realised, but she couldn't bring herself to talk about Ryan, it was still too raw. Perhaps it always would be. Instead, she changed the subject, moving the conversation along to the thing they had in common.

Their baby.

CHAPTER THIRTY-TWO

A lex picked at her food and scraped it to one side like she used to as a child, when she'd had too many sweets at her friend's house and had little appetite for dinner. She felt Henry's eyes on her, his concern palpable as he watched her nibble at a piece of cucumber. She wanted to be annoyed but she could partially understand it – she was carrying their child, responsible for it in every way while it grew inside her, so of course Henry was going to be concerned for her welfare, because her health ensured their baby's.

Another part of her wanted to ask him whether he knew what it felt like to chew food that actively made you want to throw up, food that seemed to have the consistency of cotton wool and cardboard. Or whether he'd ever experienced spooning his lunch into his mouth as he simultaneously swallowed down the acidic taste of bile.

By the time their plates were cleared away, they'd managed to cover the most pressing topics. They'd talked about the pregnancy and how often they would see each other and what their expectations were – once a week, maybe twice, they'd decided upon, and it would be strictly platonic because they had enough to be thinking about for the time being.

Alex was surprised by how easily the conversation flowed and how comfortable she felt in his presence. He'd asked her about work again and she told him she didn't know what to do. Henry told her he knew several head teachers through his job and that he would ask around, find out whether there were any vacancies. She didn't tell him about the circumstances surrounding her sudden departure from her old job; she couldn't. Ryan and everything associated with him were off limits for now.

They'd talked about money and the long list of things the baby would need. Henry told her he would help in any way she felt comfortable with and Alex had suggested they split everything fifty–fifty. Henry had agreed – he was an agreeable sort of person, she realised, but she couldn't work out whether it was because he was laid-back or whether he was simply trying to please her.

After another round of drinks Alex checked her watch. 'I'd better get going. Before the rain comes.'

'Of course, looks like we're going to get some thunder too.'

Alex slid out from the booth and Henry joined her, taking out his wallet and walking towards the bar. 'This one's on me,' he said.

'No, we can split the bill. Remember, fifty–fifty?'

'Please, let me. It's the least I can do. You're going to have to buy new clothes and things which haven't even crossed my mind. That's not to say I'm not willing to help…'

Alex forced a smile. 'Okay. Thank you.'

Henry paid and left a tip which made the waitress beam. When they got outside the grey light from midday had darkened considerably. It was almost half past two but it felt as though the night was already drawing in. Henry was looking up at the sky, frowning.

'I don't like the look of those clouds,' he said. 'Where have you parked?'

'Williamson Street. Not far.' It was the place where she'd shared her first kiss with Ryan, and when she'd pulled into a parking space there earlier that day she couldn't help but remember every little detail from that night – the way the street lights had reflected in his bright blue eyes; the way he'd brushed her hair away from her face and let his hands graze her arms; the way his mouth had felt on hers; the way he'd smelled; the way he'd tasted.

'I'll walk with you.'

'No, it's okay. I'm going to pop to a couple of shops first anyway.' She had no intention of going shopping but the idea of Henry being in a place that held such sentimental value to her made her feel strangely repulsed. She felt an overwhelming need to protect the spaces she had occupied with Ryan, to shield the memories that were all she had left.

'Baby shopping? I could come.'

'No, *me* shopping,' she lied. 'Personal items.'

'Oh, sorry, I was getting a bit carried away thinking about buying baby clothes. We should probably wait until we know if it's a boy or girl though.'

'You want to find out?'

'Yes, don't you?'

She hadn't really thought about it, much like with everything else. The twenty-week scan seemed so far in the future. 'I'm not sure.'

'Oh,' he said flatly. 'I just thought we could be more organised that way, but if you'd prefer not to know that's absolutely your call.'

Alex's gut reaction was that there were so few surprises left in life – genuine, happy, life-changing surprises – and she wanted to be the one to hold her baby in her arms and find out for herself. Some things, she thought, were worth waiting for.

'Let's think about it,' she said, deciding not to press the matter for now. 'We've got plenty of time before we need to make a decision.'

Henry nodded. 'Yes, let's think about it.'

Alex felt the first spots of rain begin to fall, light and sporadic, the thick clouds ahead moving south with the winds. Henry held out his hands, palms up, as though trying to catch the little droplets.

'I'll let you go before the heavens open,' he said. 'See you soon?'

'Yes. See you soon.'

She turned and walked off in the direction of Williamson Street. When she reached the corner, she glanced back over her shoulder but Henry had already gone, disappearing into the crowds of shoppers.

CHAPTER THIRTY-THREE

Alex woke with a clearer mind than the day before, a fog lifting, allowing her to gather her thoughts and put them in order. There'd been a storm overnight. The sound of the thunder had echoed off the trees and penetrated the house; she'd felt the vibrations of it in her bones.

She got up and showered then blow-dried her hair. She dressed in a pair of jeans and a floaty white blouse. All of her clothes were feeling snug around her expanding tummy. She stood facing the mirror, sideways on, assessing the roundness of it. It had happened quite suddenly, almost overnight, but there was a definite fullness there. A baby. *Her* baby.

She placed her hands on her stomach and closed her eyes, trying to imagine the little life growing inside. She'd looked online and found size comparisons at this stage to an apple; she tried to envisage a little fruit-sized baby growing in her belly, tiny fingers and toes, and she found she was smiling.

Alex looked out of the window. The ground was still damp from the rain, puddles cluttering the lane in front of the house, but the sky was a brilliant, faultless blue, the thick cloud from the day before a distant memory. She went downstairs to grab some breakfast – the sickness had not entirely gone but she felt that she could eat a slice of toast without heaving, which was progress.

'You look nice, dear.' Her mum was stood in her mint green dressing gown, her hair unbrushed and her eyes tired. She was leaning against the worktop, a mug of tea in her hands. As Alex entered the kitchen, Carol turned to flick the kettle on.

'Thank you. Did you sleep okay?'

'Not particularly. The storm was loud, wasn't it?'

'It was, but I liked it. Slept better than I have in a while.'

'You always liked thunder, even as a child.'

'I did?'

'Yes. You'd ask if Dad's ship would be okay and when I said yes, it would be fine, you'd turn to the window and count how many seconds there were between the lightning strike and the thunder.'

'Oh yes, I remember. You used to tell me that meant how many miles away it was.'

'There's some truth to that, you know.'

Alex frowned. 'Really? I always thought it was a myth.'

'The simplicity of how I told you to work it out isn't accurate, but there's some science behind it. I think it needs to be divided by three, then that's roughly how many kilometres away the thunderstorm is.'

Alex smiled at her mum; she never failed to surprise her. 'Wow, I'll remember that.'

The kettle boiled and Carol turned away from her, taking a mug out of the cupboard.

'Are you off out?'

'Yes, just going to pop into Nottingham.'

'Shopping?'

'Yes, I could do with some new clothes.'

It wasn't a lie, Alex did want to look for some clothes which felt less restrictive, but she also wanted to have a look around some estate agents. She couldn't stay here, living in a village that held too many painful memories; a place that was too close to the man she knew she would always love. She knew she wouldn't be able to walk down the street or take her baby to the shop without looking over her shoulder, hoping she wouldn't see Ryan or Hannah or anyone else who knew what had happened – which was just about everyone in Elwood.

'Are you meeting anyone?' There was a hopeful air to her mum's tone which Alex knew meant she was digging for information about Henry, hoping that Alex was giving it a go with the polite and handsome man who'd arrived at their house. She put Alex's drink down on the table and sat opposite her.

'Maybe.' Alex smiled, letting her mum believe whatever made her happy.

'I'm pleased for you, Alex. It'll be good for you, getting back out there.'

'Thanks, Mum.'

'Do you want some breakfast?'

'I was going to make some toast, do you want some?'

'That would be lovely.'

'Will Dad want anything?'

'Oh no, he was up in the night with the storm, I heard him making himself something to eat.'

Alex could count on one hand how many times she'd seen her dad since she'd been home, and even when their paths had crossed on the odd occasion, they'd exchanged nothing more than pleasantries. It was as though he could not understand what she was doing there, in her childhood home with her ageing parents, and Alex often wondered just how much her mum had told him.

They ate their toast and chatted about the weather and the garden and all the things which were easy to talk about, never skirting close to things that weren't. Just after ten, Alex left the house, driving into Nottingham and parking in the familiar car park on Williamson Street. The warmth had returned but it was less humid and oppressive. The storm had cleared the air and Alex revelled in the fact that all that rage and anger could equate to something calm on the other side; that something good could come from it. She hoped that would be the same for her.

She walked into the city centre, enjoying the morning sun and making a mental note of the things she wanted to do that day – new trousers, new tops, new underwear, and property research. She knew she wouldn't be able to get a mortgage on her own without a job, but she needed to feel armed with information.

Henry's offer of a place to stay had tucked itself into a shadowy part of her mind, one she didn't necessarily want to access or act upon but one that made her feel safe in the knowledge that she had a Plan B. She could stay with her parents through the newborn stage, when she knew her mum's help would prove invaluable, but she wouldn't be able to stay for long.

Perhaps she could split her time between her parents and Henry's house until she was able to go back to work. The possibilities swirled around inside her head. She needed to know what sort of properties were in her price range, and everything else could be figured out from there.

She turned a corner to head down a street lined with shops which led to the main square. There was a McDonald's on the right-hand side and the smell of bacon came wafting out into the street. Alex stopped, feeling an unexpected surge of appetite. She checked her watch – they'd still be serving breakfast. She turned into the double doors and headed straight for the automated screens to order herself a bacon roll. She was thankful to be feeling hungry for anything at all so she was happy to oblige the sudden urgency of her craving.

'Oh, hey.' A man was stood in front of her having just ordered from the opposite side of the machine. He was wearing a blue T-shirt with 'Norton's Flooring' written across it in bold white lettering. He was tall and gangly looking with shaved blond hair.

He looked familiar; Alex searched his face, hoping his name would come to her, but she couldn't quite place him.

'Vinnie,' he said, pointing to himself. 'Alex, right?'

He scratched his head, looking a little uncomfortable, and as he did she caught a glimpse of a tattoo on his inner forearm. *Arabella.* Suddenly, Alex realised where she knew him from – Henry's friend, the one who had danced with Emma.

'Oh, Vinnie, sorry, I didn't recognise you at first. How are you?'

'Good thanks, just ordered some breakfast before my next job.'

Alex suddenly felt self-conscious. How much did this man know about her? Did he know she was pregnant? That she'd slept with his friend but couldn't remember it?

'What do you do?' she asked, searching for conversation then realising he had his occupation emblazoned across his top.

He pointed at the words and grinned. 'Flooring.'

'Ah, yes. On a Sunday, though?'

'No rest for the wicked!'

'Have you seen much of Henry?'

'Not since that night.' He grinned again and it made Alex feel uneasy.

'I was very, very drunk that night, as I'm sure you know. I don't make a habit of it.'

'Well, Henry must have liked you to leave his car. Did he tell you he got clamped?'

'Huh? Leave his car where?'

'In the city... overnight.'

'I'm sorry, I don't follow.'

'He'd driven into Nottingham. He wasn't drinking so he could have driven home but he obviously had a better offer.' He laughed but seemed to cut it short, the look on Alex's face causing him to question whether he'd said too much. 'Anyway, I'd better go and listen out for my order.' He gestured over his shoulder with his thumb, towards the counter. 'Take care.'

'Wait. Just… wait a minute. Henry was sober that night?'

'Yeah…' Vinnie's tone was quiet; nervous. His eyes flitted around, looking for an escape from a conversation which had quickly taken a turn.

'What… um… are you sure?'

'Yeah, I'm sure. Henry doesn't really drink, never has.'

Alex felt the room spinning, the new information hitting her like a tornado passing through, upturning her life.

'Look, I'd better go,' Vinnie said, but as he turned round Alex quickly shouted him back.

'Vinnie, just one last thing: what car does he drive?'

He shrugged. 'An Audi,' he said, confusion etched on his face.

'What sort?'

'An A3, I think.'

'A hatchback?'

He shrugged. 'I guess.'

'What colour?'

He paused for a second before answering, thinking.

'Grey.'

CHAPTER THIRTY-FOUR

Alex was back in her car, struggling to breathe against the weight of what Vinnie had told her. It felt as though it was compressing her chest. Invading her heart and lungs. Filling her with a dread so deep and twisted that it hurt parts of her she never knew existed – the place between her ribs, the hollow spaces inside, the ones which surrounded her tiny baby. The baby whose father had lied so unimaginably that she couldn't fathom how she hadn't seen it before now. She held a hand to her tummy. She needed to protect it – its innocence and fragility, its delicate little fingers and toes.

She gripped the steering wheel with her other hand, trying to offset some of the tension which coursed through her veins, pumping into her limbs with a ferocity she hadn't experienced before. She needed to move. To hit something. To refuse to be still. But at the same time, she couldn't. She couldn't control herself while the weight was so immeasurable and her thoughts were so chaotic. She felt sick and dizzy and fragile and weak. She felt helpless.

She took out her phone and called the only man capable of making her feel like more than her mistakes. She didn't allow herself to consider the repercussions. She didn't allow herself to question whether what she was doing was right or wrong or whether it fell into the grey space between the two. All she could think about was that she needed him, to hear his voice and know that there was something in this world which could make her feel better than she did right at that very moment.

'Hello?' His voice was quiet against the noise of heavy traffic in the background.

'Ryan?' Her voice was thick with tears she couldn't hold back.

'Alex? What's wrong?'

'Oh God, oh God, everything. Everything's wrong.'

'Where are you?'

'Nottingham.'

'Whereabouts?'

'The car park. Williamson Street.'

'Wait there – I'll come to you.'

Alex sobbed into the phone, tears seeping into the space between her cheek and the screen, dropping into her lap. She rested her forehead against the steering wheel.

'Alex? You still there?'

She heard a car engine starting up.

'Yes, I'm still here.'

'I won't be long, I'm not far away. Stay there, okay?'

'Okay,' she cried. 'Okay, I'll wait for you.'

She heard the line fade to silence as Ryan hung up. She dropped the phone into her lap.

I'll wait for you.

She wondered whether Ryan realised just how much meaning was behind those simple words.

CHAPTER THIRTY-FIVE

Alex tried to calm down while she waited for Ryan. She wanted to be able to talk to him, to provide him with facts rather than emotions. To ask him for his help as someone who loved her; someone who wanted nothing but the best for her. She wondered what his reaction would be.

She hadn't seen him angry before but she felt sure that was what he would feel – anger towards Henry, the man who had lied his way into her life. The man who Ryan had watched lead Alex from the taxi to her home; the man who he'd hoped could provide her with what he could not; the man who had made him realise that what he had with Alex wasn't just a fling.

She thought about Henry's car, the grey hatchback she'd seen several times before, sitting in wait, hiding in shadows. She couldn't prove it was him, but she knew it with a certainty that made bile rise in her throat. Had he been following her?

She thought back to the scratch on her car, from the day she'd been to the Peak District with Ryan. Then to the flowers… and the word SLUT on her windscreen. The times she'd felt sure someone was watching her; the times she thought she'd heard someone right outside her door. She felt so confused. So angry. So scared.

The chaos in her mind made her shoulders tense as the tears slowed, crawling down her cheeks as though they too were giving up. It was too much – too much for one person to feel, too much for one person to make sense of.

There was a soft vibration on her lap as her mobile buzzed. She picked it up expecting an update from Ryan and was repulsed to find Henry's name displayed on the screen instead – *Henry – may or may not call*. A message, one single sentence that just an hour earlier would have seemed quite trivial.

How's your Sunday going?

Alex was clenching her jaw, her teeth pushed tightly together, staring at the screen with wide eyes full of rage. Movement to her right pulled her attention away and she was relieved to see Ryan's car beside her. He was looking at her, his eyes full of concern. She got out of her car and into the passenger side of his.

'What's happened?' he asked, before she'd even closed the door. 'Are you okay?'

She nodded as another tear escaped and she wiped it away. Ryan unclipped his seat belt and leaned over towards her, pulling her into him.

'Alex,' he whispered, his breath in her hair. 'Talk to me.'

'I don't know where to start.' She sobbed into the sleeve of his T-shirt, a fresh wave of tears erupting.

He pulled back and looked at her, taking her hand. 'At the beginning,' he said. 'Start at the beginning.'

'I don't even know where that is. I don't know anything anymore. I've fucked up. I should never have gone out drinking that night.'

'What night?'

'The night you saw me come home with that guy.'

'Alex, we've talked about this – it's none of my business what you–'

'It is. I want it to be your business. I... I was hammered. I don't even know if it was just alcohol.'

'I don't understand. What do you mean?'

The thought had come to Alex almost immediately, Emma's words coming back to her like a bad dream. *I was tipsy but I was nowhere near as drunk as you. In fact, I've never seen you like that before.* Had Henry slipped something into her drink?

'I've just seen one of his friends. He said Henry was driving that night. He was sober! I was hammered. Or drugged... or *something*. I don't know, but it's all blank... all of it!' Her words were tumbling out of her, fast and chaotic. It was as though she needed to dispel the trauma, to shift some of the weight of it.

'We slept together but I don't remember anything. I don't have any memory of it: it's all black. All of it! But he must have known what he was doing. He *must* have, because he told me he was drunk too, and that he didn't remember that night, but he lied. He lied! He was driving!'

'Okay, okay, calm down, take some deep breaths.' Ryan gripped her hand a little tighter and looked into her eyes, trying to anchor her.

'He's been following me too,' she said, unable to stop talking, unable to calm down. 'I keep seeing a car, a grey one. The night you and I met outside the woods it was on Beck Lane. Then I've seen it other times too. I asked Vinnie what car Henry drives and he said a grey Audi. It's his car, I know it!'

'Who's Vinnie?'

'The guy I saw! Henry's friend!'

Ryan's face had changed. His jaw had tightened, his lips pressed tightly together. His breathing seemed harsher and his eyes darted around the car as though looking for an answer.

'That...' He sat back in his seat, burying his head in his hands and exhaling heavily. 'Son of a bitch!' He punched the steering wheel, hard and sudden, and as Alex looked at him she could see that his eyes had filled with fury. He took some deep breaths before turning back to Alex who, faced with Ryan's emotions, had managed to calm her own. His anger comforted her.

'The scratch on my car...' she said, leaving her words hanging for a moment. 'The knock at my door the night you were at mine... the flowers... being followed... it all makes sense now. It all makes sense!'

'But... the scratch on your car... that was *before* you met him, wasn't it?'

'I knew him before, kind of. Barely at all, really, but he remembered me. He approached me in Nottingham that night and knew my name. He'd been at a course I attended back in January.'

'January? You think this has been going on since *January*?'

Alex considered it for a moment, trying to remember when it all began. On Valentine's Day, she'd received a card addressed to the school. It was blank inside except for a single kiss. It had sat uneasily in her mind for a while, completely out of the ordinary to anything she had ever received before. It had been delivered with the school mail with her name on the front and a first class stamp.

She'd suspected it was from the dad of one of her old students, a man who'd lost his wife a couple of years earlier while Alex was teaching his daughter. She'd been attentive and kind, supporting them both and going above and beyond. She'd wondered if he'd misconstrued it as something more. He'd always made a point of coming over to speak to her at the school fayres or plays; anything that brought the school community together. Had she read it all wrong? Had it actually been from Henry?

'Nothing sinister until…' She paused, suddenly realising when it all began to change. 'Until you and I started seeing each other. The first time I noticed his car was after you'd dropped me off the night we met. Then the scratch on my car was after we'd been out together. Then there was writing on my windscreen after I'd met you at the woods.'

'Writing?'

She nodded. '*Slut.*'

'Jesus.' Ryan was shaking his head. 'I had a nail in my tyre at work the next day. I remember it because I was already feeling pretty crap about everything, but I changed the tyre and didn't think anything more of it. Maybe it was nothing but…'

'Maybe it was *him.*'

'I'll take you to the police station. I can tell them what I saw that night. We can go through everything.'

'No.' Her voice was firm and it seemed to catch Ryan by surprise.

'What do you mean? You have to report him, Alex. He can't get away with it.'

'I can't.'

'Alex, he… he *raped* you.'

She closed her eyes at the word, fearing it would make everything more real. 'I know what it was. I *know.* But what would it look like to the police? I was all over him in the bar – Emma told me. People would have seen. There'd be cameras.'

'Who's Emma?'

'My friend, the one I went out with. We were drinking – how would I prove he wasn't too?'

'The guy… Vinnie… he could tell the police…' Ryan began, but she could tell from his tone the futility in his words.

'His *friend!*'

'We have to *try*, Alex. We have to report him.'

'I got in a taxi with him! You saw me go inside with him, you tell me – did it look like I was letting him in under duress?'

Ryan shook his head almost imperceptibly. 'That doesn't mean you consented, Alex.'

Alex ignored him, unable to take in what he was saying. 'Not to mention the fact that I was later found to have been sleeping with the father of one of my pupils! It would all be dug up, all of it! I can't go through that, I can't!' Alex wasn't even sure her words were making sense anymore, but she shouted them anyway, as though filling the car with noise would push the reality away. 'I've been out with him since. For a meal. If I accused him now...' She put her head in her hands.

'Alex...' Ryan began, but instead of words a silence settled, so heavy Alex was sure she could feel it. It crept between them and filled all of the empty spaces with the harsh reality that Ryan could not save her from this. He could not provide all the answers. 'I'm sorry,' he whispered. 'I'm sorry I didn't intervene that night. I'm sorry I...' He inhaled sharply. 'I'm sorry I watched him follow you inside.'

'You weren't to know. This isn't your fault.' Alex heard herself speak but her voice no longer sounded like her own. It was factual and detached and she wondered whether she'd hit her limit on emotion, her mind and body agreeing to shut down to save her from anything else. She felt exhausted all of a sudden and as she turned to face Ryan she had to fight an overwhelming urge to crawl into his lap and close her eyes.

Ryan looked away from the spot on the windshield he'd been staring at, lost somewhere she could not go. She could see that he was crying, his eyes darkened by the truth, haunted by the fact he could not rescue her.

'I don't know what to do,' she said. She wanted to tell him that she needed him, that she wanted him to leave Hannah and fight for Mia, to be by her side and make everything okay; but she couldn't do it, not like this. She couldn't ask him for the world as hers lay broken.

Ryan reached out his hand and wiped away the stray tear that was beginning a slow descent down her cheek. He took a deep breath but it was shaky, broken by a cry he was trying to hold back. Alex knew he was trying to be strong for her, and her heart broke because of it.

'I love you,' he whispered. 'I wish that could solve everything. I wish that were enough.'

CHAPTER THIRTY-SIX

Alex drove home slowly, in no particular hurry to get there. Her head ached and her tummy felt unsettled, poisoned by new information. She'd said goodbye to Ryan then continued to hold on to him for long enough that her shoulders had begun to ache. Ryan's phone had rung on two separate occasions, one after the other. He hadn't looked at the display, they both knew who it was.

Alex hadn't wanted to let him go, as though parting from him would be signalling the start of a new future, one that looked bleak and uncertain; one that didn't contain Ryan. When they'd finally parted, she'd been surprised to hear him say he would check how she was the following day, that he'd call her in the afternoon from work and they'd talk some more. She'd nodded and he'd kissed her on her cheek before she left.

She pulled up outside the house but didn't go inside for a while. Upstairs, the curtains were closed to her dad's bedroom, hiding him away from the world. She felt she understood him now more than she ever had, his need to withdraw. Her mind drifted back to being a child at Christmastime. She'd been given a speaking part in her school play and had been rehearsing for weeks to remember the lines off by heart. The night before, her dad returned home and she greeted him at the door. He scooped her up into his arms and held her there, his mouth nuzzled into her hair, kissing her head over and over again.

'Daddy, it's my school play tomorrow! I know all my lines!'

'That's my girl!'

Carol had ushered her upstairs to bed where she'd lain awake rehearsing in a whisper to the dark. The following morning her dad had stayed in bed. She'd jumped in beside him and felt his warmth under the covers, his rough hand resting on her cheek.

'Morning, baby.'

'Daddy, it's my play today!'

'Good luck, sweetheart.'

She'd frowned. 'Aren't you coming?'

'Daddy needs to sleep today, it's been a long few weeks out at sea.'

She'd sloped from his room and found comfort in her mum, in her stability and consistency. Over the years, she'd found herself doing that more and more until, over time, she stopped having any expectations of her father at all. It was as though the distance had become so vast, the crevasse filled with so much, that they would never find a way to bridge it.

The front door opened and Carol stood there, waving her inside. Alex took a deep breath, trying to steady the emotion that had resurfaced at the sight of her. She couldn't help but think of her dad in that moment and how, sometimes, you avoid those closest to you out of fear they'll detect what's really wrong. She got out of the car and walked inside.

'There's been a delivery for you,' Carol said. She looked happy – the juxtaposition was so severe it felt palpable. Alex had to fight the urge to run away.

They walked into the kitchen, the sound of the kettle boiling in the background. In the middle of the kitchen table was a huge bouquet of flowers. Lilies. They were wrapped in gold paper and

Carol had placed them inside a tall crystal vase. Alex swallowed down an acidic taste of bile, fighting a wave of nausea. They were exactly the same as the ones she had received before. The ones she had wrongly thought were from Ryan. She looked at the card, handwritten in neat cursive.

Thinking of you. Henry x

'Alex, what's wrong?' Her mum's expression changed, concern flooding her features.

'Oh, Mum,' she cried. 'I'm in a bit of a mess.'

Carol stepped closer towards her and placed her hand on her shoulder, firmly, letting her know that she was there. 'Is it about the baby?'

Alex looked at her, eyes full of surprise.

'I know you're pregnant, Alex.'

'How?'

'I'm your mother. I *know*.'

Alex's cries suddenly ceased as the shock took over. Hearing her mum say the words she'd been desperately trying to cling on to was a relief; horrifying yet comforting in equal measure. She felt her knees weaken and her barriers come crashing down. Carol drew back a chair and guided her to it, taking some of the weight Alex had been struggling to carry.

———

Alex told her mum everything, even the parts which hurt her to say. Carol didn't interrupt, she understood that Alex needed to offload in a way that was fast and fierce and unstoppable, a way that couldn't be stalled with requests to clarify or expand, but her eyes belied her silence, giving away the things that bubbled within.

When Alex finished talking her mum looked away for a

moment, down at her hands that had not let go of Alex's. She seemed either lost in thought or in an inability to think – Alex couldn't decide which.

'Mum?' she said. 'Say something, please.'

Carol looked up at her and a single tear traced the half circle beneath her eye. 'Alexandra, I wish you would have come to me.'

'I couldn't,' she cried.

'You could have. You can always come to me. My love and support isn't conditional, you know that. Now,' she said, her voice firm, 'we need to think about what we're going to do.'

The use of the word *we* filled Alex with warmth. She wasn't an *I* in this anymore; she had her mum – someone to help guide her, to take some of the pressure.

'I can't go to the police, Mum, I can't. I *won't*.'

'No, I see that. I've been a woman in this world for long enough to understand the injustices in it.'

Alex was surprised, once again, by her mum; by her quiet strength and wisdom, unassuming and yet full of something powerful. Alex found herself calming under her mum's direction, relishing someone else taking control. Someone she trusted so completely.

'This man… Henry,' she said, as though his name left a bitter taste in her mouth. 'Tell me everything you know about him.'

CHAPTER THIRTY-SEVEN

Alex's phone vibrated from her bedside table. The sky outside was trapped between light and dark and it was impossible to tell whether it was the end of the day or the start of a new one. Over a week had passed since Alex had seen Vinnie in Nottingham; over a week since the truth she thought she knew had disintegrated and changed into something ugly and repulsive.

Henry had tried calling her every single day, and she suspected that was who was calling her again. He'd taken to ringing her at all hours; texting her ten, twenty times in a row. His early unassuming nature had quickly transformed into persistence which now teetered towards harassment.

Her mum had contacted him, early last Monday before the working day began. She'd told him Alex had miscarried. Henry had turned up at the house, uninvited and unwanted, and her mum had turned him away, telling him she needed to rest. Alex had stood hidden from view in the kitchen, her back against the wall, listening.

'When did it happen?' he'd asked.

'Over the weekend,' her mum had replied, trying to keep the information vague enough not to trip up over the lies.

'The weekend? Which day?'

Her mum had stuttered then, her uncertainty so clear that Alex had closed her eyes, knowing he wouldn't buy it.

'Sunday.'

'You don't sound very sure. Why has no one told me until now?'

'We've had other things on our mind.'

'But you're sure it was Sunday?'

'Yes,' her mum confirmed. 'It was Sunday.'

'Morning? Or afternoon?'

'I'm... I can't remember. Around lunchtime, I think.'

Alex had the unnerving feeling as she listened that it had been this piece of information which had confirmed to Henry that it was all a lie; that she hadn't miscarried and that their baby was still thriving, a perfect little secret she intended to keep for herself.

She imagined his car creeping past the entrance to the Williamson Street car park. She imagined him sitting there, watching as she cried, as she called Ryan in a panic then waited for him to arrive. Had he been watching them?

Her doubts about the plan working were momentarily eased the following day when he'd sent flowers, a little card attached telling her, once again, that he was thinking of her. She believed him. She believed that he did little else *but* think of her. After the flowers he'd sent her a card, hand delivered, telling her he was there for her should she want to talk. She'd ripped it up into countless tiny pieces then thrown it into the bin.

The following day, there was a cuddly bear in a gift bag attached to the front door handle. Her mum had taken it from her and dropped it straight into the wheelie bin outside, as though its very presence in the house was simply too much.

By the end of the week the gifts had stopped, replaced instead by his scepticism. He'd turned up at the house on Friday, and then again the next day and the next day and the next. It was now Tuesday. He'd been round to the house in the early evening and she knew he would be there again the following day. They'd taken to not answering the door, to keeping the curtains drawn and hoping that he'd get the message.

He'd taken to pounding his fists so heavily against the doors and windows that Alex felt sure they would break under the strain. Her mum had tentatively broached the topic of reporting him on a couple of occasions, her shoulders hunched and her face full of worry. But, despite hating what this was doing to her mum, Alex refused. She'd been over and over it in her mind and she came to the same conclusion every time: she couldn't go through that – she knew that reporting him would open her up to the kind of scrutiny she could not withstand, and she felt a deep-rooted fear that *she* would ultimately be blamed.

Alex's eyes found the alarm clock next to her bed and the red digits which told her it was just after 10pm. She rubbed at her eyes, sleep clinging to them. So far that day she'd had eighteen text messages. They'd started off harmless enough, as always, but throughout the course of the day they shifted gear, carrying a sinister tone that came close to threatening.

> Please, Alex. Just talk to me. We can work this out.

> What kind of a mother pretends to have a miscarriage?

> We could raise this baby together, Alex. We could put this all behind us.

> Think about what happened at the school. With Ryan. A child was harmed because of you. You need help raising this baby.

Alex felt his desperation, frightening and unhinged. She grabbed her phone, fully expecting to see yet another missed call from Henry, but it wasn't his name there at all – it was Ryan's. She sat up in bed, her heart jumping. She'd talked to Ryan only once since she'd seen him in the car park. He'd rung her the following day from work, checking in, seeing how she was doing and whether she'd changed her mind about going to the police. He'd told her he was sorry again and the pain had carried through the phone and landed in her heart.

'You have nothing to be sorry for,' she'd told him. '*Nothing.*'

'Then why does it feel like I do?' She'd heard him breathe heavily down the phone. 'I wish I could be there with you. *For* you,' he'd said.

'But you can't.'

'No. I can't.' There was so much regret in his words.

'Ryan, you were there for me when I needed you.'

There was a long stretch of silence before Ryan spoke. 'I love you, Alex.'

Before she could reply, he'd hung up.

She hadn't expected to hear from him again, at least not for a while. She held on to the belief that it was simply the wrong time and that, at some point in the future, it might not be. One day, Mia would be older and able to make her own decisions, and enough time would have passed that Henry would feel like a distant memory; a nightmare she could hardly recall.

Alex thought for a moment about whether she should call him back at this hour, hesitating when she thought about the risk of Hannah being there, but before she could come to a decision the screen lit up again.

'Hello?'

'Alex?' Ryan's tone was full of urgency, one single word enough to let her know he wasn't calling to chat but rather to tell her something she already knew she didn't want to hear.

'What's wrong?'

'Fucking hell, Alex, he showed up at my house.'

'Who did?' she asked, though she already knew.

'Henry, that fucking bastard. He showed up at my house!'

'What! Why? What did he say?'

'He waited until Hannah had left for work then he casually knocked on my door and asked if I'd seen you. Said he was concerned and thought maybe I'd heard from you. I told him no, I hadn't. I wanted to fucking lunge at him, Alex, that smug bastard just stood there as though he hadn't got a care in the world.'

'Jesus, I'm so sorry, Ryan.'

'That's not even the beginning. He went on to ask how Mia is. Said he'd seen her leaving school for a hospital appointment. I thought he was bullshitting then I remembered, she had to go for a check-up on her arm – Hannah had taken her. He knew the time and date, Alex.'

Alex swallowed hard, trying to find the right words and failing. 'Oh God,' was all she could get out.

'I stepped outside and shut the door, told him he needed to leave.'

'Did he?'

'Yeah, he left, but before he did he took a step toward me and said something about how important family is, and how he'd do anything to protect his.' There was a long pause; Alex could hear Ryan's breath down the phone, quick and heavy. 'I think he's dangerous, Alex. I think he's really fucking dangerous.'

Alex brought her knees up to her chest and held them there, cradling them against her thrashing heart, her forehead resting against her knees. She could feel the roundness of her belly.

'Jesus, Ryan, what have I got you into?'

'Alex, do not let him do this. Do not let him make you feel that you've done anything wrong. He's a psycho, a fucking psycho. I want to kill him, Alex. I want to fucking kill him.'

Alex had never heard Ryan sound like this. She'd never heard him lose his temper or swear or trip up over his words. But there was a truth to what he said, raw and uncontainable, a truth that made her believe every word.

CHAPTER THIRTY-EIGHT

The rain came again, disguised by the dark but relentless nonetheless. Alex had lay there in bed, her phone clutched in her hands and her heart hammering so hard it caught her breath, pummelling the same unyielding patter, refusing to calm. It was as though it was trying to force her to move, to do something. To act. But she couldn't.

She'd said a reluctant goodbye to Ryan who had told her he needed to think – that they *both* should think about what to do; where to go; who to talk to. He'd skirted around the option of going to the police again which didn't seem like an option at all to Alex; what it felt like was another layer of complication which would ultimately end in more distress. She had to think about her baby. She had another life to protect, one already more important than hers.

Just after 2am, Alex gave in to the futility of trying to sleep, knowing that she was fighting a losing battle. Her mouth felt dry and her throat sore. She decided to go downstairs for a glass of milk; heartburn had started to rear its head this past week, stinging her chest and burning the back of her throat. She flicked on her bedside lamp, found her robe then padded barefoot downstairs.

She was surprised to find she wasn't alone when she entered the kitchen, and the silhouette of a man sat at the table made her take a step backwards at first, panicked, thoughts of Henry fresh and raw in her mind. Then her dad looked over his shoulder and smiled briefly, nodding by way of acknowledgement.

'Didn't mean to startle you,' he said. He was dressed in a pair of navy plaid pyjama bottoms and a plain white T-shirt, his grey hair swept back from his face. It was longer than Alex had seen it in a while. As a child, she was used to seeing him with close-cropped hair on his head and at least a month's worth of growth in his beard, but now it seemed as though he'd traded one for the other. His facial hair was still there but was trimmed, while his hair had grown almost to his shoulders. He ran his hand through it, a glass of water on the table in front of him.

'What are you doing up?' she asked. She went over to the fridge and took out the milk, pouring herself a glass.

'Couldn't sleep.'

Alex took a seat opposite him. 'Me neither.' They were sat in the dark, the only light coming from the single bulb out in the hallway.

'Not like you to be up.' He took a drink from his glass and Alex did the same, the coolness of the milk easing the fire she felt was simmering in her chest.

'No, I don't suppose it is.'

He seemed to take a long deep breath, the kind people take before they have something important to say. Alex looked at him – her dad, the slight man in front of her who had once seemed so strong, his skin now thin and paper-like, as though his transition had already begun, on his way to becoming a ghost.

'Your mum told me everything,' he said, still not looking at Alex but down at the table in front of her. Alex didn't say anything. 'I've met a few men like this Henry chap in my time, nasty pieces of work, all have something in common.' His eyes moved up to her. 'They don't quit. They don't like to lose. Can't take it.'

Still, Alex didn't respond. She was listening, taking in his words, trying to let them land, but she was exhausted.

'I don't sleep very well – curse of being old, I suppose, but every time I've been up this past week, every time I've looked out that window, out onto the lane, he's been there. Watching.' Alex felt an icy shiver run up her spine, into her head and flood freely through her body. She saw the skin on her arms pimple, felt her hands shake. 'Your mother noticed him first, but she didn't want to tell you – always trying to shield you from the things you need to know.' He paused for a moment. 'He sees me. He even waves sometimes. He won't leave it here. He won't let you be.'

Alex wanted to cry again, to expel the emotion, but she found she couldn't. 'I know, Dad. I know.'

'Then what are you going to do about it?'

That was the difference between her parents: her mum wanted to share her problems while her dad made it clear they were her own. As a child, it had been an odd mix, her mum wanting to swoop in and save her while her dad insisted she go it alone.

'Don't worry, Dad, I'm not asking for your help.'

'That's not what I'm saying, Alexandra.'

'Then what *are* you saying? What am I going to do about it? You want to know? I haven't a clue, okay! I haven't a clue!'

'Calm down.' His voice was flat, emotionless, and Alex felt a rush of anger towards herself for ever expecting anything more. 'You know what you have to do,' he said. 'You know there's no other way. Your mother... she means well, always has, but she's never been very good at setting people free.' Alex looked at him, frowning, wondering what it was he was trying to convey. 'She'll support you and love you because it's all she knows how to do, but is that really what you need? Is that really going to help you?'

'It's better than nothing.'

He looked away, his chin dropping to his chest.

'I have never been a good father or a good husband, Alexandra. I have always loved you, but I have not always deserved you.' He looked back up to her, his eyes seeming clearer than they had just moments earlier, an intensity in them that Alex could not remember seeing before. 'Sometimes, walking away takes great strength, the type I have never had myself but the type I have seen in you your whole life.'

'You think I should walk away?'

'No,' he said, clearing his throat. 'I think you should run.'

CHAPTER THIRTY-NINE

Somewhere in the early hours, Alex's dad had slipped an envelope under her bedroom door, her name scrawled across the front. Before the sun rose, she opened it, confusion causing her to tear it apart, the contents falling to the floor. She picked it up. Inside was a piece of paper with Registers Of Scotland written across the top. Her eyes searched for information, struggling to make sense of it. Under a section headed 'Description' she saw an address. Number 4, The Cabins, Forest East, Inverness.

Alex stepped quietly out onto the landing, listening for clues as to whether her mum was up. She heard a cupboard shut downstairs, the fridge open and close. She knocked lightly on her parents' bedroom door but didn't wait for a response. Her dad was sat on the edge of the bed, still dressed in his pyjamas, his hair unkempt and his eyes staring out of the window.

'He's there again,' he said, then he got up and closed the curtains. 'He got out of the car and tried the front door this morning. I'm going to get someone round to tighten up the security.'

Alex felt her heart plummet. She knew things were escalating fast and she was angry at herself for ever being naïve enough to think that they wouldn't. From the doorway, she could hear her phone vibrating against the nightstand in her room.

Her dad turned to her. 'Ah, you got my note.'

'This isn't a note, Dad, it's the title deeds to a cabin. In Scotland!'

'Yes, that's right. And all in someone else's name.'

'I don't understand. Why have you given me this?'

'I had a good job,' he said, sitting back down on the bed, his hands clasped in his lap. 'Good pension. You know me, I don't spend any money, and I don't travel. I have no use for a cabin in the middle of nowhere, but it seems like you might.'

'Whose cabin is it?'

'It's mine.'

'But the name says Morven Smith.'

'Yes, that's right, but she won't be using it.'

'Dad!' She had to struggle to keep her voice down, mindful of her mum pottering around downstairs. 'Who's Morven Smith?'

'I guess you could say she was the great love of my life, and that's not something I say with pride, but it's something I have come to terms with. We fell in love in the summer of '87, but by the time I returned home to your mum, I found out she was pregnant. I tried to make it work with both your mother and with Morven, but of course that could never happen. Not in the long term.'

'So... so you chose Mum?'

'I chose you, Alexandra, but unfortunately you got the broken-hearted version of myself, my mind always partially elsewhere.'

'What happened with Morven? Why do you have this?' Alex thrust the deeds out in front of her.

'Morven got tired of waiting for me to be a man, to make a decision. She met someone else.' He shrugged as though it were of no significance but his eyes told a different story. 'She had kids and moved to Australia. The cabin was cheap back then, and we both had good jobs, we thought it would be a good place to hide away from the world. I went to meet her one day; I'd been out at sea for a couple of weeks then travelled up north for the weekend. It was December, just before the millennium.'

'Jesus, Dad, it lasted that long?'

He nodded. 'She'd left. She'd took her things and left me a letter, and those deeds. Said she couldn't do it anymore.'

Alex sat down on the bed beside him, their shoulders touching. It was the closest she'd been to him in as long as she could remember, in more ways than one.

'When I think back to what you were like when I was little, I remember you always seemed sad. I thought... I thought it was us. It never seemed like we were enough.'

'You were more than enough, Alexandra, more than enough. But part of my heart was with a woman I could never be with. I never once regretted my decision to stay, because I got to see you grow up. And I loved your mother, in my own way.'

'But not in the same way you loved Morven?'

'I'm afraid not. You can't steer your heart in a different direction, it has a mind of its own, as I'm sure you know.'

She thought of Ryan and wanted to tell her dad that yes, she understood. Then she thought of Mia and couldn't help imagining her in thirty years' time, having the same conversation with a forlorn Ryan.

'I don't know what to do.'

'You do.' He put his arm around her and she let herself be held, her head dropping to his shoulder. 'You've always known your own mind. You've always been strong and courageous and all the things I lacked.'

'If you could go back and do it again, would you do things differently?'

He seemed to think about it for a long time; so long that she wondered whether he was ever going to reply. 'I don't think there was ever a choice I could have made that would have left my heart whole, and if it was going to break for someone, I would rather it have been for a woman than my daughter.'

———

When Alex returned to her room, she found twelve missed calls on her phone. She closed her eyes before looking at them, mentally preparing herself to once again see Henry's name on the screen. She'd called her network provider twice to change her number and, both times, she'd hung up halfway through, scared of the repercussions. If he couldn't carry on calling her, if he thought she'd taken further steps to block him from her life and their baby, what would he do next? What was he capable of?

She unlocked her phone and, sure enough, Henry's name sat at the top of the list, nine missed calls in the space of twelve minutes. But they weren't all from him: three were from Ryan. He'd called fifteen minutes earlier, three times in a row. She immediately tried phoning him back. He picked up on the first ring.

'Alex?'

'Yes?'

'Are you okay?' Then, before she could answer: 'Where are you?'

'I'm at home. At my parents'. Why?'

'He was outside again, in the early hours, just watching the house. Then about an hour ago he sped off like a lunatic.'

Alex didn't need to ask who he was talking about. She felt her chest tighten. 'He's outside here now. On Beck Lane.' Her tone defied the situation; as though she were delivering news inconsequential to both of them, and she realised that she'd begun to accept the reality of the situation. She felt numb.

'What? Jesus, Alex. I think we need to do something. We need to call the police. We can't keep pretending this is going to go away.' Ryan was speaking with urgency, the words rushing out of him. He sounded scared and Alex understood that the fear wasn't for himself. It was for Mia.

'I'm leaving,' she said, the words out of her mouth before she realised she'd made her decision.

'What? What are you talking about?'

'There's nothing keeping me here anymore. I need to disappear for a while.'

'Alex...' he began, but she stopped him.

'Ryan, you're right. We can't keep pretending this is going to go away. But, maybe, without me around, you can go back to living your life without fear. I never wanted any of this.'

'Hey, don't... don't do that.'

'Do what?'

'Try to take on some of the accountability.'

'If I hadn't gone out that night...'

'We could drive ourselves mad thinking about what-ifs. If I hadn't have left you waiting... If I hadn't have turned up at your house that evening or kissed you in the car park...'

Alex closed her eyes, memories flooding back.

'Where are you going to go?' he asked.

'I think it's best you don't know.'

'Alex, you can't run away from this...'

'Can't I?'

'You need people around you. Your family. You're going to need help when the baby comes.'

'I know that. I know.' She paced her room, thinking. 'One day, this will all be over.'

'What do you mean?'

She stopped pacing and took a long deep breath. 'Goodbye, Ryan.'

She hung up the phone and lay down on her bed and, as she did, she felt a little flutter inside her tummy. It could have been nerves, or a lurch of something else, but Alex put her hand on the firm roundness of her belly and chose to believe it was her baby. A sign she was doing the right thing.

CHAPTER FORTY

Early the following morning, while the sun was still an amber flicker on the horizon and the birds were loud in their solitude, before her mum had begun to stir or the cars had started to clog the roads, Alex crept downstairs with a single suitcase and a rucksack. Her dad was waiting for her, a flask of tea in his hand which he passed to her along with a brown envelope packed full of something Alex suspected was money.

'You'll need some cash,' he told her. 'To get you settled. Been stood empty a while, it'll need a few jobs doing I suspect.'

'Am I doing the right thing, Dad?'

'We both know you are.'

'But... Mum.' Tears stung Alex's eyes. She'd left her a letter explaining everything, the words flowing on paper which she knew would be too hard to say to her face.

'You've explained everything in the letter?' Alex nodded. 'I'll make sure she understands, and it's not like we won't see you again. Just let things settle. We'll sort this out, okay? Who knows, maybe we'll join you up there, sell this old place and start afresh.'

'I'd like that.'

They stood at the front door, her dad in his dressing gown and slippers.

'I've checked,' he said, sensing her apprehension. 'The lane is clear, but keep your wits about you, just in case. Double back on yourself a couple of times, make sure you aren't being followed. Here, let me help you out with your things.' He took the suitcase from her and opened the door, carrying it out to her car to avoid the sound of the wheels dragging against the gravel.

Alex pressed the button on her keys and her dad opened the boot. When the car was packed they stood in the shadowy light of dawn and looked at each other. Alex watched as he put his hands in the pockets of his robe, his uneasiness growing in the face of their goodbye.

For a moment, she was able to see him as a man – not her father or her mother's husband, but a man in his own right, broken and full of fault lines, a man who had tried to do the right thing when there was no clear path, a man who had spent his life loving someone he could not have, while struggling to show his love to those that he'd stayed for.

'Bye, Dad.'

He nodded, tight-lipped, then turned back towards the house for a second as though deciding whether he should stay to watch her leave.

'Give us a call, when you're settled. On the new phone. And take care of yourself, and the baby.'

It was the first time he'd mentioned the baby, the reason behind everything.

'I will.'

'Drive safe.' He stepped back, away from the car, and she got inside with the flask of tea and her rucksack and started the engine. She turned the car slowly on the drive, a flock of birds taking flight from an overhanging sycamore as the tyres crunched against gravel. She took a last look in her rear-view mirror at the shadowy silhouette of her dad, his arm raised in a wave, then she pressed down on the accelerator and turned right onto Beck Lane.

She flicked on the headlights, golden beams cutting through the greyness of the morning that was shrouded in low cloud, masking things which she hoped were not there. It wasn't until she was on the motorway, the skies clearing and the roads flowing, that she felt her shoulders relax slightly, her jaw unclenching and her heart rate easing.

She tried to visualise the miles stretching out as she drove, relishing the space she was putting between herself and Henry, while knowing it would never be enough.

CHAPTER FORTY-ONE

AFTER

Alex stood back and forced herself to be still. Her body was rigid and it seemed to claw at her breath, diminishing its effectiveness, her lungs never getting enough air. She clenched her hands into fists and forced the tension down to her fingers, her nails cutting into the palms of her hands.

The door opened slowly, grinding on its hinges, and the floorboards creaked under the weight of someone shifting just beyond. Alex moved her jaw back and forth, forced her face to relax, then she smiled.

'Alex.' He let out a heavy breath and straightened his glasses.

'Hi, Henry,' she said, her voice taking her by surprise; she'd managed to sound confident, her tone welcoming.

'I knew I'd find you eventually.'

'I'm glad you did.'

He frowned. 'You are?'

'I knew you would, sooner or later. I had to get away from Ryan, I hope you can understand that.'

Henry's eyes narrowed suspiciously, but Alex was sure she'd seen the flicker of a smile at the edges of his mouth. A lie was much easier to believe if you *wanted* to believe it.

'He was obsessed with me, Henry.'

'You didn't seem to have a problem with him when you were meeting him out in the Peaks, or at that car park in Nottingham, or out by the woods.'

'No, I loved him once.' She saw Henry's eyes flash with anger. She quickly continued. 'But when I realised what he was like I tried to end things, but he made it so hard.'

He shoved his hands into his pockets. He looked different to how she'd remembered him and she was relieved to find she saw no resemblance at all to the beautiful boy who lay fast asleep in the bedroom.

'I want to know about the baby.' His voice was firm, demanding information rather than requesting it. 'The baby you took from me.'

Alex smiled, the force of it hard against her cheeks, the feel of it unnatural. 'He's sleeping, but you could take a peak if we're quiet?'

'*He*? I have a *son*?'

Alex nodded then turned towards the door, pushing it open with the palm of her hand. He was still fast asleep in his green bodysuit, a little fluffy bunny beside him which her parents had brought with them the previous month.

Henry hovered behind her and she could feel his breath in her hair, the heat of his chest against her back. She didn't move, she didn't want to let him into the room any more than she had to. She turned and put a finger to her lips then gestured back outside.

Henry removed his glasses and rubbed at his eyes. 'I can't believe I have a son. What's his name?'

'Sonny.'

He considered it for a moment before smiling. 'I like it. Sonny. My son, Sonny.' He laughed as though it were the funniest thing he'd ever heard.

Alex put her finger to her lips again, indicating to be quiet. He obliged.

'You shouldn't leave him alone, you know. I know you weren't out there very long but it's still irresponsible.'

Alex felt her nostrils flare but quickly recovered, nodding. 'Yes, I suppose you're right. But I don't have any support around me here. No one to help watch him.'

'And whose fault is that, Alex? Hmm? Who ran away?'

'Henry, I didn't have a choice. Surely you can understand I needed to get away from Ryan?' It hurt her to say the words and they seemed to leave a bad taste in her mouth, but she knew she would say just about anything to appease Henry.

'I could have come with you, so you didn't have to struggle. I could have kept you both safe.'

'I realise that now. But I panicked.'

Henry scratched his head, thinking about it for a moment, so Alex took the opportunity to move the conversation away from her leaving.

'I'll make us a drink,' she said, walking toward the kitchen area and flicking on the kettle. She wanted him to follow her but he remained by the couch, hovering between her and Sonny. It felt like a threat; a barrier. She had to fight the maternal urge that felt so strong, the one which told her she should not be allowing this man near her child.

'Coffee?' she asked. 'Or would you prefer tea?'

'Coffee's fine. I've got to say, Alex, this is not what I expected.'

'No? What did you expect?'

He walked towards her and leaned his forearms on the kitchen worktop. Alex felt her heart calm slightly. 'I saw Vinnie,' he said, a grin on his face which made Alex want to throw the contents of the kettle all over him. But she didn't, she carried on as she was, putting instant coffee into the two yellow mugs.

'Sugar?'

Henry nodded.

'I have to admit, I was quite upset about what he told me.' She kept her eyes averted, concentrating on making their drinks.

'Yes, I thought you might be. I'm sorry I lied.' He spoke in a manner that would suggest he'd lied about something trivial, leaning casually on the counter watching her pour water into the mugs. Alex stopped herself from saying anything, because there wasn't a single thing she could find to say in that moment that wouldn't have jeopardised the whole plan. 'Do you believe in love at first sight?' he asked.

His question halted her. She stopped stirring their drinks and looked at him quizzically, wondering whether he'd completely changed the subject or whether this were somehow linked to his attempt at an explanation.

'I don't know.'

'Well, I do. I loved you from the first moment we met, back in that old church hall in the middle of nowhere, remember?' Alex nodded. 'I knew I loved you, and I knew that, given the chance, you could love me too. There was a connection – something...' he searched for the right word, 'electric. So I found out where you worked and did a little digging. I managed to catch you in Nottingham that night and, well, I couldn't believe you remembered everything so clearly... the fact that it had snowed.' He smiled.

Alex could recall mentioning this to him in The Garden Room, but her memory of the snow was linked to a bad date she'd experienced, not to him – the man she had struggled to remember. She wanted to tell him, to watch her words get under his skin and cause him pain, but she couldn't. She remained calm. Stoic.

'I knew then that you'd felt it too. That we were destined to be together. It was just a matter of time and... perseverance.'

'Were you following me?' She tried to sound conversational rather than accusatory, as though she were simply curious, maybe even a little flattered.

'I guess you could call it that. I was *watching* you. Waiting for the right opportunity. I just needed the chance to ask you out, because you'd rushed off so suddenly after the training event.'

'Yes, yes I had.' She grabbed the milk from the fridge feeling as though she were floating on air, not quite connected to her own body anymore.

'Obviously, I would have preferred us both to have remembered our first night together, but I can assure you it was... very special.'

She had to turn away. It was too much, too repulsive. She thought she might actually be sick if she heard any more. She pretended to rummage around in the cupboard for the sugar.

'I hated seeing you with him, you know. *Hated* it. It was so obvious you weren't right for each other but you continued to see him, even after our night together.'

'I know. I don't know what I was thinking.'

'He has a wife, Alex. And a daughter. Poor little Mia.'

'I know, Henry. Like I said, I don't know what I was thinking.' She stopped herself from saying any more.

'I was surprised when you went out for the day together. Very brazen of him, all things considered.'

An image suddenly appeared in her mind: the scratch down the side of her car.

'Did you...' She cleared her throat, giving herself a moment to adjust her tone. There was too much accusation in it, she needed to soften her words. 'Did you key my car, Henry?'

He smirked. 'Yeah, I'm sorry about that. I didn't want to do it, but I was so angry.' There was a flash in his eyes, an echo of the anger he'd felt as he remembered. It changed his whole face. Alex felt a bolt of fear run down her spine. She focused on her breathing, trying to stay calm.

'So, how did you find me?'

'Your mum and dad,' he said simply. 'They still keep an old-fashioned address book by the phone.'

'Henry,' she said in a mock-scalding tone. 'You went in their house?'

She could feel her heart pounding; her blood pulsating in her ears. The adrenaline was pumping through her body but she had no use for it, it wasn't time for fight or flight.

He shrugged. 'I needed to find you. I needed to find my son. Tell me about him.'

She put the sugar in their coffee and stirred it. She pushed one of the mugs across the worktop and Henry took it.

'He's... perfect.' She turned to the fridge and took out a plate full of pastries, placing it on the worktop between them. 'Freshly baked,' she said. 'And nut free. The health visitor said to be careful with Sonny in case he's inherited your allergies.'

'That makes sense,' Henry said, helping himself to a croissant. 'Thanks.' He took a bite.

'He's seven months old,' Alex told him. She took a long drink of her coffee and Henry did the same, his eyes full of anticipation, hanging on her every word. 'He's just had his first tooth through so we've had a lot of sleepless nights recently.'

'I wish I could have been here to help.' Henry scratched at his neck and took another drink of his coffee.

'He loves his food, especially bananas and sweet potato. And he rolls over all the time, so I can't take my eyes off him!'

'Is he crawling?' he asked, taking another bite of his croissant.

'No, not yet. Trying though. He loves being outside, watching the water and the animals.'

Henry cleared his throat, coughed, then raised his hands to his neck, scratching again.

'I've decorated the spare room,' he said. 'I went with yellow, since I didn't know whether I had a son or a daughter. But it's all ready for him.' He coughed again, then his eyes looked from the croissant to Alex and back again. His breathing was becoming shallow and laboured. Alex noticed his lips had started to swell and little red hives were appearing all around his mouth, his skin reddening and his eyes filling with horror.

He dropped the croissant, the ones Alex baked twice a week, always at the ready ever since her parents had last visited around a month earlier; the ones which had ground-up nuts of every kind weaved into the pastry. He tried to smell the golden flakes on his fingertips but he was struggling to take in air so instead he picked up his coffee and threw it, directly at Alex but falling short as she stepped back. He fell to the ground and, as he did, his hands went into his trouser pocket, searching.

Alex walked round to the other side of the counter and crouched down next to him. 'You raped me,' she said, her voice quiet, not wanting the tone of it to reach her baby's ears. 'You poured petrol through my parents' door. You tried to intimidate them into telling you where their daughter and grandson were, and when they wouldn't, you broke into their home.' She put her hand into his pocket and pulled the epi pen from his grip. 'Did you really think I would let you anywhere near my son?'

Henry's whole face was swollen, his eyes sunken against the purple tinged skin, his glasses straining. She pulled them from his face and, as she did, he grabbed her wrist. She let him; he was weak, the life draining from him, his last breaths loud and frantic.

She leaned down so that her face was close to his. 'I wish he was Ryan's.'

CHAPTER FORTY-TWO

S onny sat in his high chair sucking on a carrot, smiling and laughing as Alex pottered around the cabin, collecting their things, packing them into bags and boxes. She'd acquired so much stuff since being there – how was it possible that someone so small could need so many things?

It had been a month since Henry had died; a month since she'd called the ambulance in tears and told them how she'd tried to help him; how she'd administered the epi pen but it had been too late. She did not tell them that she'd stuck it in his leg twenty-five minutes after she'd felt his pulse fade to nothing. It was a tragic accident – she'd had no idea he had a nut allergy and he had failed to mention it as they sat down to breakfast, waiting for her son to stir.

'Right, I think we're all set, Sonny! Let's get you cleaned up.' She pulled him from his high chair and wiped his face on his bib. 'Are we going to go and see Nanny and Granddad? Yes we are!'

She'd timed the drive home so that he would hopefully sleep for the first couple of hours, then she would make a stop before carrying on home. She would be staying at her parents' until she was settled; her dad had painted the spare room blue, erected a cot and a new set of drawers. Her mum had sent her the pictures.

It had been Alex's idea, the nuts. It had sat in a shadowy part of her mind since before Sonny was born, a weapon to be used should she require it. When her parents had visited the previous month, her dad had pulled her to one side and told her that Henry had poured petrol through their letterbox. He still watched the house, still turned up demanding information.

Her mum had taken to ordering their shopping online, avoiding the outside world and everyone in it. She looked frail, as though old age had suddenly caught her in its grasps, her skin paper-thin, almost translucent.

Her dad had managed to track down Henry's ex-girlfriend, who was indeed living in America, just like he'd told her. What he'd failed to mention, however, was that she'd fled out of fear. Rihanna Gibbs' initial reluctance to speak to Alex's dad had soon waned when he'd explained the circumstances. She told him about the abuse she'd endured. The jealousy and control. She'd met Henry through work, in the same way he'd met Alex, then he'd turned up at a yoga class she took every Saturday.

They'd begun dating, happily at first, until things started to happen which made her question everything. A colleague of hers had been assaulted outside work, a colleague who she had previously dated and remained on good terms with. Then Henry started turning up while she was out with her friends, and she would struggle to recall how she'd got home. She tried to leave him but it soon became clear to her that it would not be possible to simply walk away. She needed to run. Far and fast.

'It's escalating, Alexandra,' her dad had said, his back to the cabin, his eyes set on the loch. 'Things are different for him this time because of the baby. He won't let you go the way he did Rihanna. We either go to the police, or we sort this out ourselves.'

'And what about Rihanna?' she'd asked. 'Will she come forward?'

Her dad had shook his head. Alex couldn't blame her: she'd escaped, and she didn't want to jeopardise her freedom.

'Nuts,' she'd said simply. 'He's allergic to them.'

Her dad had nodded, just once. 'You'll be ready for him?'

'I'll be ready,' she'd said.

'I'll see to it that he's able to find you.'

And that had been it: the conversation that led to the death of the man who had upturned their lives. She'd looked over her shoulder at her mum sitting on the decking, Sonny asleep on her knee, and Alex had felt a renewed strength. She had people to fight for.

It had been a relief when Henry had taken the croissant, a relief that she hadn't had to earn his trust first, to go through the motions of the day, to allow him to hold her son. After his death, she'd disposed of the homemade curry from the freezer, the sponge cake and the cookies, all laced with ground-up nuts. She threw it all away, thankful that he'd taken the first thing she'd offered; that he'd never had to touch a hair on Sonny's head. Or hers.

She strapped Sonny into his car seat then put the last of their bags into the boot of the car. Before she got in she looked out over the loch, at the place she'd called home for over a year, the place that had hidden her until she was ready to be found.

She pulled her phone from her pocket and typed out a text.

I'm coming home.

THE END

ACKNOWLEDGEMENTS

Thank you to the wonderful Bloodhound Books team for their continued support and guidance, particularly Betsy for seeing something in my writing and giving me an incredible opportunity to bring my books to life. Thank you also to the rest of the team: Fred, Abbie, Tara and Kate, and to my wonderful editor Morgen; it has been a pleasure to work with you again. And thank you to Ian for the early insight into the book; your suggestions were invaluable.

Thank you to my first readers: Caron, Beth, Nicki and Abby. You are all very busy people and I'm so grateful that you make time to read my work in its early form and offer feedback.

Thank you to my wonderful family for the support and enthusiasm and for always believing in me.

To my husband: for the countless times you've jumped onboard a lengthy conversation about a character I have just made up – thank you. You understand that, to me, they're real people, and they're important to you because of it. Thank you for being a calm presence when I (often) need it. I love and appreciate you.

A shout out to my children: thank you for making my days loud and unpredictable. You are my greatest creations and my wildest adventure. I love you both very much.

A NOTE FROM THE PUBLISHER

Thank you for reading this book. If you enjoyed it please do consider leaving a review on Amazon to help others find it too.

We hate typos. All of our books have been rigorously edited and proofread, but sometimes mistakes do slip through. If you have spotted a typo, please do let us know and we can get it amended within hours.

info@bloodhoundbooks.com

Made in the USA
Columbia, SC
04 August 2023

21263434R00150